His For A Week

RUINED

THIS BOOK WAS DONATED
TO THE HONESTY LIBRARY
AT WESTON FAVELL
SHOPPING CENTRE

EM BROWN

Published by Wind Color Press
Copyright © 2019 by Em Brown

All rights reserved under International and Pan-American Copyright Conventions

This is a work of fiction. Names, characters, places, and incidents are either the products of the author's imagination or are used fictitiously, and any resemblance to actual persons, living or dead, business establishments, events, or locales is purely coincidental.

By payment of required fees, you have been granted the *non*-exclusive, *non*-transferable right to access and read the text of this book. No part of this text may be reproduced, transmitted, downloaded, decompiled, reverse engineered, or stored in or introduced into any information storage and retrieval system, in any form or by any means, whether electronic or mechanical, now known or hereinafter invented without the express written permission of copyright owner.

RUINED

CHAPTER ONE

"Clean it again," was the general manager's reply to my co-worker, Rosa, when she explains that the penthouse suite, which no one had used, had been cleaned two days ago.

"The room is going to be so perfectly clean, so spotless and shiny, that anyone would be comfortable eating off the damn toilet seat," Mr. Danforth continues.

Rosa and I exchange glances. Whoever is checking into the penthouse of The Montclair, a boutique hotel nestled on San Francisco's Nob Hill, has to be somebody important for Mr. Danforth to get his hair extensions in a knot.

"Well, what are you waiting for?" demands Mrs. Ruiz, the housekeeping manager. "Mr. Lee will be here in a few hours!"

I raise my hand with some hesitation because Mrs. Ruiz is not likely to welcome my reminder.

"You said I could leave early," I say. "I was going to go over to Berkeley and talk to the financial aid officer."

Sure enough, she looks annoyed, and Mr. Danforth looks at her as if I just asked to triple my pay instead of taking off an hour early. She closes her eyes and sighs, but I can tell she remembers that she agreed yesterday to let me clock out early today.

"Can you take care of that tomorrow?" she asks. "We're already short-staffed. I need you to work the Grand Pacific Suite."

Tomorrow is difficult because I will either have to miss my class at the community college or make it into work late, but Mr. Danforth's stare is boring holes into me, so I nod.

As Rosa, Maria, Sierra and I take the elevator up to the twelfth floor, I ask, "Who is Mr. Lee? *Quíen es Señor Lee?*"

"*No sé,*" Maria answers with a shrug.

I actually picked up a little Spanish back in North Carolina, where I'm from, as there is a growing Hispanic population there, but having lived in California for ten months now, and worked alongside many Spanish-speaking women, I can actually string more than two words together.

"I was afraid to ask," Rosa says. "It's like we're supposed to know already, but I never heard the name before."

Sierra has earbuds on and probably didn't hear my question. I'm not sure she would know anyway. I push the housekeeping trolley out of the elevator.

"Do you think they want us to replace the clean linen, too?" I wonder.

Maria shrugs again as Rosa opens the double

doors of the suite. The penthouse at The Montclair is insane. It's the only penthouse I've ever actually seen, and I bet all penthouses are amazing. But at nearly 4,000 square feet with floor-to-ceiling views of the city, I can't imagine anything more luxurious. It's bigger than the apartment I live in with two other women out in the Sunset District on the west side of the city. And there's a frickin' grand piano in the foyer. Do most rich people play the piano?

And the price tag on this place would take me three months' worth of income, pre-tax, to afford. And that's assuming I don't need my wages for anything else, like tuition for my classes at City College of San Francisco, MUNI fare, and food.

"We should just *say* we cleaned the place," Sierra remarks when we enter the suite. A beautiful blond, Sierra's just buying her time at the hotel until she makes it big as a model. "I mean, why the hell are we cleaning the place twice?"

She plops down on a sofa wide enough to seat eight people and grabs a magazine from the glass coffee table, but Maria takes the bedroom and Rosa heads into the kitchen.

Sierra shakes her head. "Lame."

"They're just hardworking," I say.

"They're probably afraid ICE will ship their asses back to Mexico if they don't jump at everything management says."

"I think Maria's from Venezuela."

"Whatever. You going to be as lame as them, Veronica?"

"Virginia," I correct. "I'll take the bathroom."

Sierra rolls her eyes and starts flipping through the magazine. Part of me wants to have words with her, but I agree that it's silly to repeat a job that's already been done. I decide to leave it alone.

With its Jacuzzi bathtub tucked into a bay alcove, a separate waterfall shower, double artisan sinks, and marble flooring, the bathroom is bigger than my bedroom. I manage to finish scrubbing, wiping, and mopping the already clean bathroom before Mrs. Ruiz rushes in.

"He's here early!" she exclaims. "Finish up! Quick!"

I grab the cleaning supplies and replace them onto the trolley. I manage to wheel it out of the suite as Mr. Danforth steps off the elevator and stands aside to let a man wearing perfectly pressed slacks and a button-down shirt pass. With his jet-black hair gelled back, perfect tan, and designer sunglasses, he looks like a movie star. But more than the way he looks, it's the way he moves that has me rooted to my spot. I'm guessing he's only six feet at most, but he carries himself as if he's much taller. I've never seen anyone with such smooth, almost elegant confidence.

As the men pass by with the bellhop bringing the luggage behind them, Maria and Rosa lower their eyes, as if they're not worthy of meeting the eyes of royalty.

"Hi, Mr. Danforth, Mr. Lee," Sierra greets.

Mr. Danforth frowns at her. She hasn't gotten the memo that housekeeping isn't to be seen or heard.

Mr. Lee doesn't acknowledge Sierra, though he seems to see her. Me, too. Though it's hard to tell through his sunglasses, our gazes meet briefly and his feels *intense*. It seems as if he stares at me several beats longer than what I would consider normal. I lower my eyes and oddly feel like I need to bob a curtsy. When I look back up, the men have entered the suite and closed the doors behind them.

"Omigod, he's so much hotter in person," Sierra exhales, fanning herself.

"Was that Mr. Lee?" I ask.

She nods.

"Is he some famous businessman?"

She stares at me, "That's Tony Lee. The Lees own The Montclair, dipshit."

****

Between studying and working, I haven't had a chance to replace my broken umbrella, so of course it rains. And it's not just a drizzle but the steady kind that comes in at an angle and gets your feet wet even if you're under an umbrella.

As I stand under the canopy of the entrance to

The Montclair, I do my best to consolidate my backpack, a copy of *Fifty Shades Darker* that I checked out from the library to read on the MUNI ride back to my apartment, and a water bottle underneath my jacket. It's too dark to tell if there's any break in the rainclouds, so I step out from beneath the canopy, ready to rush as fast as I can to the MUNI station, and promptly slip on the wet pavement.

The ground is even harder than I expected, and I lay there, stunned.

Within seconds, firm arms lift me up, and I'm cradled in security before being set back on my feet beneath the canopy. Embarrassed, I turn around to thank whoever assisted me.

Only it's *him*. And the words get stuck in my throat. I'm not sure why I find the guy a touch intimidating. So his family owns the hotel. That doesn't necessarily affect me. Mrs. Ruiz knows I'm a good employee. And it's not like I haven't come across rich or famous people working at the hotel before. People dressed every bit as nice as Tony Lee, though this man rocks a suit and trench coat like no one else.

"They're regular people who piss in a toilet just like everybody else," I recall Lila, my adoptive mother, once saying, "and their shit stinks just as bad."

Finding my nerves, I say, "Thanks. Guess I

shouldn't be in such a hurry."

He picks up the water bottle and *Fifty Shades* from where they fell. Noting the barcode and ripped plastic wrap on the book, he says, "Didn't know people still used libraries."

He's got an accent I can't place, though he speaks English in a relaxed manner.

"You like the book?"

"I haven't gotten very far," I reply as I brush the dampness from my back, hoping there's not a big wet spot on my behind, before receiving the items from him.

"But you've read the first one."

I blush, realizing he knows about *Fifty Shades*. It's not exactly the kind of book I would trumpet in front of my boss' boss' boss—or whatever he is in relation to a maid. I mean, the book's not Brontë or Dickens.

"I did," I admit and get ready to take my leave. "Thanks again."

"Wait."

He spoke in a low easy tone, but it was a command he expected would be followed.

"You don't have an umbrella."

"Mine broke yesterday."

Last time I buy a three-dollar umbrella from the drugstore.

"Where are you headed?"

"Just to the MUNI station," I answer.

He nods to the limo waiting at the curb. "I'll give you a lift."

"Oh, you don't have to. It's not that far."

For some reason, I'd rather not take a ride from the man. But he's already taken me by the elbow and turned me towards the vehicle while the chauffer opens the door. Mr. Lee either didn't hear me or he's choosing to ignore me. I give him the benefit of the doubt that it's the former and find myself climbing into the car. I've never been in a limo before. My friends had rented one for senior prom, but I never got to go with them because my date didn't want to chip in the money to pay for one, so we arrived at prom in his used pickup.

Mr. Lee takes a seat beside me, then changes his mind and sits diagonally across from me, the farthest he can be from me.

Do I smell bad? Maybe I reek of cleaning products. But despite the embarrassment, I'm glad for the extra distance between us.

Virginia Mayhew Porter, what has gotten into you?

"MUNI station," he tells the driver before pulling out his cellphone. He dials, then starts talking in a foreign language. Chinese, I'm guessing.

He's staring at me with that same intensity he had in the hotel hallway. Except he's talking away, so maybe he's not looking *at* me, just in my direction.

The limo turns off Eddy Street onto Powell Street

where stairs on the sidewalk lead down to the train station. Mr. Lee pauses his call.

"Thanks for the ride," I say as the chauffer opens my door.

Mr. Lee says something in Chinese to the driver, who hands me the umbrella he is holding.

"Thanks, but I don't—" I begin.

"Keep it," Mr. Lee tells me.

It's not an offer. It's an order.

I take the umbrella, say my thanks again, and watch him return to his call before the driver closes the door. No goodbye or "have a good night." I'm not sure if it's a cultural thing or it's just that I'm not important enough to merit a final word. But he did give me a ride and an umbrella. And for that I am grateful, or I would have been soaking wet. Still, it would have been polite if he had asked me my name.

On the MUNI ride home, I don't end up reading *Fifty Shades*. Instead, I relive what it felt like to have his arms around me.

CHAPTER TWO

"You gonna join us tonight?" my roommate, Talia, asks me before she heads out to her job as a barista at a local coffee shop. She tells me as soon as there is an opening, she'll put in a good word for me. Serving coffee is a lot nicer than cleaning hotel rooms. Her worst day involves dealing with obnoxious customers who chew her out because she accidentally used 2% reduced-fat milk instead of skim. Mine involves emptying wastebaskets that someone has vomited in, pulling bloody or cum-soaked sheets off the bed, and having to fish out tampons that didn't flush down the toilet.

"I've got to study for my economics class," I reply as I rush around the room to get dressed. I want to make it to the financial aid office at Berkeley as soon as they open so I'll only miss half my morning class. It's better I miss class than miss work. I need the money, and everything in the San Francisco Bay Area is pricier than it is back in North Carolina.

Talia, who also takes classes at City College, leans her curves against the doorframe. She has the sort of body I wish I had: long, lean legs, full B-cup breasts, and a nice swell to the hips. A woman's body. Even though I turned twenty-one a few months ago, I feel like I have the body of a teenager, and I've resigned myself to the fact that my breasts will forever be locked in A-cups.

"Don't you ever want to get laid?" she asks. "Like, finally lose your virginity?"

I blush. I'm not going out of my way to preserve my virginity or anything. I'm not saving it for the love of my life. But in between moving across country to find my birth mother, applying for college, and trying to save money to send to Lila, losing my virginity hasn't been a priority.

"Maybe I'll join you tomorrow night if y'all go out," I say.

"You know, losing your virginity is something you've got to get out of the way. Then you get to really enjoy sex. It doesn't matter who that first guy is 'cause nine times out of ten, it's never Mr. Right."

"I know. I just don't want the first guy to be a total loser."

"I can set you up with my cousin Tyler. According to Alexia, he's really good in bed."

Alexia has the other bedroom in our place, and given that she has a different boyfriend every month, she's probably qualified to judge.

"I'll think about it," I say.

Talia perks up and takes herself off the doorframe. "You let me know when. I'll hook you up."

I remember meeting Tyler once. He seemed nice. And he was good-looking. If I had to lose my virginity, I suppose he would be a good one. Although I'm not terribly romantic, I would like my first time to be memorable, in a positive way. But maybe Talia's right. Maybe you just have to get it out of the way, like a vaccination, so you can get on with the better parts of your life. I heard the first time is not that enjoyable for most women anyway.

After leaving the house and catching the BART train to Berkeley, I make it to the financial aid office fifteen minutes after they open.

"I'm going to be honest with you, the chances of receiving grants or scholarships are low," the financial aid officer tells me, "but you can definitely qualify for some student loans. The federal loans will have the best rates, and maybe you can supplement that with some work-study. The pay is usually fairly competitive."

I stifle my sigh of disappointment and ask him, "How many hours of that can I get?"

"It varies but most students I know work four to eight hours a week."

"That's it?" There's no way I can cover rent and send money back to Lila working just eight hours a week. "Can I get two work-study jobs?"

"You don't want to overdo it, or you won't have enough time to study. The academics here at Berkeley are quite rigorous. Plus, college is about having some fun, too, young lady. You have to have balance."

I return his encouraging smile, but in truth, what he calls balance seems like a luxury to me. Even though Lila insists I shouldn't worry about her and that I have to go live my life, I can't help but feel guilty that I'm not back in Durham with her and my adoptive younger brother, Andre, a sophomore in high school. The best way to assuage my guilt is to send them money so that Andre can play AAU basketball. His coach wants him to attend this special basketball camp attended by a lot of college recruits. Apparently, unless you're the next LeBron James or Kobe Bryant, it's not enough to just play ball for one's high school; one has to play in the special tournaments off season to get noticed. The camp costs several thousand dollars, and there's no way I can help out enough if I attend UC Berkeley.

I make it to my morning class later than planned because I couldn't resist hanging out on campus for a bit. I love the Berkeley campus and the college town that surrounds it. It reminds of Chapel Hill, where Lila went to college. While I love the hustle and bustle of students going to and from class and all the different eateries and hangouts that surround the school, my favorite part of the Berkeley campus is the creek that runs through it, shaded on both sides by tall trees and greenery. It's like someone plopped a small piece of the forest right in the middle of all the large buildings of concrete and glass.

After sitting through the last hour of my morning classes, in which I'm distracted, thinking that maybe I should look into enrolling in a California State University school instead of Berkeley, I rush over to The Montclair. The umbrella Mr. Lee gave me yesterday came in handy as it started to rain on my walk over, but I plan to return the umbrella with a note of thanks.

I work the tenth and eleventh floors before taking a break and sit down to eat a turkey sandwich I bought from a Starbucks I passed on the way in. Making my own sandwiches would be a lot more cost effective, but when I come home from a long day of work and classes, I don't feel up to going to the grocery store. Plus, since I don't have a car, I'd have to get a ride from one of my roommates. Or I can Uber it, but that probably makes it a wash compared to buying a sandwich on the go.

"And my agent says this guy is willing to pay *twenty thousand* if you're a virgin," Sierra is telling Tracy, a receptionist who works in the front lobby. She also attends City College.

I sit at the other end of the table in the staff room from them and open my economics textbook to read while I eat my sandwich.

"Holy shit!" Tracy replies. "I *wish* I had my virginity still. I mean, for twenty thousand dollars,

I'll pretend to be a virgin."

"You can't pretend that shit. They'll do an inspection."

"They can tell by looking?"

"You've never looked at yourself in the mirror?"

"Not down there."

"The hymen's pretty easy to see. At least mine was. After I lost my virginity, it wasn't there anymore."

"I was told you can break your hymen riding a bike."

"Well, even if you're not a virgin, you can still make like a thousand dollars *per night*."

"No way! Why would a guy pay that much? I mean, it's got to be pretty easy to find a hooker for a lot less than that."

"Because these men are rich. And maybe they don't want some trashy disease-infested streetwalker." Sierra slid a business card over to Tracy. "That's my agent's number. Call him if you're interested."

I try to understand the supply and demand curves in front of me, but my mind can't get over the number Sierra had thrown out. Twenty thousand dollars. To have sex with a virgin? That's crazy. Like medieval crazy. What's so special about having sex with a virgin? The guy would have to be some pervert or pedophile to get a high from deflowering a woman.

Twenty thousand dollars. That's eight months of pay if I worked full time. That would cover a full year of tuition and fees at Berkeley and some room and board.

My mind starts reeling. All for just one night of sex? What is my virginity worth to me?

Sierra and Tracy leave the staff break room to go outside to smoke. I finish my sandwich, and as I leave the table, I notice that the business card Sierra had slid over to Tracy is on the floor. Tracy must have dropped it. I pick it up and note the name of Dan Pullman, Pullman Model & Talent Agency. I pocket the card to give to Tracy.

The thought of having sex with a stranger in exchange for money makes me queasy. Though Lila only made it to church with me and Andre sporadically, it's not how I was raised. Plus, it's illegal. Even in California.

But damn. Twenty thousand dollars is a lot of money. I might never have a chance to make that much in one go. Not unless I win the lotto, and that's not likely to happen. With twenty thousand dollars, I could definitely afford to buy a quality umbrella.

CHAPTER THREE

"Do you know much about Tony Lee?" I ask Judy Park, an older woman of Korean descent who is working Maria's shift today. She and I spread new sheets over the king-size bed in the penthouse. All the sheets in The Montclair have a thread count of a thousand, which I'm told is what makes them so soft, but the ones in the penthouse suite have a thread count of eighteen hundred.

"His family very rich," Judy replies.

I smooth the wrinkles off the flat sheet, wondering what it would be like to sleep in sheets this soft. "Is he from China?"

Judy nods. "He Chinese."

"I didn't know there were Chinese people that rich," I say. Growing up in North Carolina, most of the Asian folks I come across are engineers or doctoral students at the universities. They don't dress or look like Tony Lee.

Judy arches a brow. "The Lees, they in the Forbes 500. China has more billionaires than any other country except U.S. And that not include Hong Kong billionaires."

"Does he come to the hotel often?"

She shakes her head. We finish the bedroom, and I go back outside to retrieve the umbrella from the trolley. I look about the living room to see where I should place the umbrella. I don't want it to be overlooked, but I don't want it to be too obtrusive either. I decide to lean it against the coat rack next to the door. That way he can grab it on his way out. I jot a thank you on a Post-it and stick it on the umbrella.

As I stand up, I hear male voices in the hallway. Rosa is still working on the bathroom, and we haven't done the living room and dining room yet.

"You want, we come back later, Mr. Lee," Judy offers as the man enters.

He wears a light colored three-piece suit, and I'm surprised that taupe can look so good on a man, but against his complexion and black hair, the color works well.

"You can finish," he tells Judy as he takes off his coat. His vest hugs his body, accentuating the V-shape of his upper body. He glances at me but takes no further notice as he makes his way to the bar.

"Martini, dirty," he says to the older gentleman who came in with him.

"Good memory," replies his companion, taking a seat on the sofa. "So you gotta make nice with Drumm, eh?"

"That's what my brother sent me here for," Mr.

Lee replies. "It's a job my father and brother think I can't fuck up too badly."

I wipe down the dining table as quickly as I can so that we can be out of their way sooner rather than later.

The other man chortles. "Still, I'm surprised Jean-Jacques's not out here himself. Seems a pretty important relationship since Drumm's father could very well be the country's next president."

"Jean thinks Drumm and I can hit it off."

Lee hands the man the martini but only has a glass of water for himself.

"To be honest, I think Eric Drumm is a twit—which is not to say that I think you are as well. Maybe your father and brother think you'll do better 'cause you're closer in age to Eric."

I think Eric Drumm is about thirty years old. I'm not used to features like Lee's, and he looks like he could be either younger or older than that. For some reason he *feels* older. Again, it's the way he carries himself. Or maybe it's because Drumm reminds me of a college frat boy based on what I've seen of him in the news.

"How long are you going to be with him?" the older man asks.

"Drumm invited me to spend a week with him. He wants to show me where he plans to develop a golf course and resort hotel."

The men talk other business while I finish wiping

down everything, dump out the wastebaskets and put new trash bags in them. Luckily, Rosa had taken care of the vacuuming first, so I'm wrapping up when Lee seems to be addressing me.

"Why is that here?"

I turn around, unsure that the question is directed at me, but he's looking at me with those dark eyes of his. He doesn't seem pleased, but maybe he's just always on the serious side. I wonder if maybe I had dropped some trash while taking out the wastebaskets, but he glances over at the umbrella.

"Oh," I say, "thanks for letting me use it yesterday."

"I told you to keep it."

"I thought it was a loaner."

"Did you get a new one?"

"No..."

He raises his brows.

"I thought you or your driver might want it back," I say, refusing to feel like an idiot for returning the umbrella.

"You don't think I can get another umbrella?"

I don't know what to say. I *do* feel like an idiot. Of course he could get another umbrella. Hell, he could probably get a million umbrellas if that many could be had.

"Take the umbrella," he instructs.

Like, now?

Reading my mind, he says, "Now. And I don't want it back. Do you understand? You're not going to prosper in life if you don't know how to receive things."

Umbrella in hand, I feel like a chastened child. He didn't have to be so patronizing. I was only trying to be courteous.

He turns back to his companion, having clearly finished with me.

Rosa has emerged from the bathroom, and we pack up quickly and leave quietly.

"He gave you his umbrella?" Judy asks me as we head to the elevator.

"He saw I didn't have one yesterday," I reply.

"You lucky. My daughter would dream to be his girlfriend."

"He's not married?" Rosa inquires.

Judy smiles broadly, shaking her head, and I think that she might have dreams of her own concerning Mr. Lee.

"I was trying to return his umbrella, and I think I upset him," I think aloud.

"Can I see the umbrella?" Rosa asks as if she expects to find it jewel encrusted.

I'm glad to have the umbrella later as it keeps me dry on my walk to the MUNI station after work. On the ride home, I get a text from Talia that she received a letter from the landlord informing us he's raising the rent after our lease is up in two months.

Dang. I'm already paying two hundred dollars more a month because Alexia's roommate moved out, and we haven't found a replacement to split the rent four ways instead of three.

"You've got to go to Berkeley," Lila tells me when I call to update her on what the financial aid officer told me. "It's a damn good school. 'Course, I always dreamed you would be a Tarheel like me, but you can't pass up an opportunity like this. It's not easy getting into Berkeley, and you did it."

"Andre's coach thinks he's good enough to get a scholarship," I say as I sit down at the dining table in my apartment and sort through the mail that's mine.

"We're talking about you, Ginny. I was thinking about some extra work I could pick up to support Andre's basketball so—"

"But you work enough hours as it is," I protest. Lila does foster placement for the county social services department. That's how she came across me and Andre. I had been with several different foster families, and Andre had been in a home. She has more cases than the county can pay her for, and I know she donates a lot of her time.

"This is your time. Your future. Don't give up on it."

Before hanging up, I assure Lila I won't make any hasty decisions. I open my credit card bill to see that I've racked up another hundred dollars in interest. Dang. I've only been paying the minimum for the last few months, and at this rate, I won't be able to pay off my credit card until long after I'm dead.

I slouch into the dining chair and stuff my hands into my coat pockets. My hand connects with the business card I have yet to return to Tracy. Pulling it out, I stare at it.

Twenty thousand dollars. Is that for real?

I consider the kind of trouble I could get into and shove the card back into my pocket.

"I raised you better than that," I can hear Lila saying.

But what if...

I picture Andre going to this basketball camp and getting a scholarship, Lila working extra hours in between taking medication for her frequent bouts of arthritis and heartburn, and me enrolled at UC Berkeley, getting to stroll by Strawberry Creek every day, taking classes from world-famous professors, attending events like football games. Maybe Andre would visit me, and I'd take him to see the men's team play.

Suddenly, it's a simple decision.

I pull out the card.

CHAPTER FOUR

This is real.

I lay motionless on the examining table as the woman inspect me between the legs. I pretend I'm getting my annual wellness checkup. This woman inserts a gloved finger into me. It's uncomfortable, but so is the speculum used by gynecologists.

The woman takes off her gloves and tells me I'm done.

I sit in the reception area of the Pullman Model & Talent Agency, which I half-expected to be located in an old building with no central air and in one of the less savory parts of the city, like the Tenderloin, given the nature of its extracurricular activities. But the office is nicely appointed and the furniture looks new. Headshots of beautiful women and men adorn the walls. I notice the photos of women outnumber the men two to one.

Forty minutes later, a middle-aged man with a receding hairline enters the office. "Virginia, eh? Dan Pullman."

As I shake his hand, I wonder if I should have provided a fake name instead.

"Can I get you coffee or tea?" he asks.

"Maybe just water," I answer. He doesn't come across particularly sleazy, but I've only just met him.

He opens a mini fridge and pulls out a bottle of water for me. "So how did you come across my info, Virginia?"

"A co-worker of mine is a model with your agency."

"Yeah? Who's that?"

"Um, Sierra."

He smiles. "Sierra is great. If she were just a few inches taller, she would be working actual modeling gigs."

He looks me over from head to toe and now the sleaze starts to show. "Nice. I like what I see, Virginia. I think you'll go for a great sum. You've got that innocent girl-next-door vibe. How old are you? Eighteen? I can't take you unless you're at least eighteen"

"Twenty-one."

"You got proof of that?"

"My driver's license."

"Good. All you got to do is fill out some paperwork and wait for my call."

He walks over to a desk and pulls out several sheets of paper. It's as if I'm applying for representation from his agency.

"Is it true that I'll be paid as much as twenty thousand dollars?" I ask as I receive the paperwork.

"You have to be chosen by a client first, but I had a model of mine just last week make thirty thousand. She had just turned eighteen. The younger the better. But you look like you can pass for eighteen."

My stomach turns, and I begin to have second thoughts. Even though Talia said losing one's virginity is just something to get out of the way, I have the feeling that a woman always remembers her first time. Do I really want my first time to be with a lech who likes jailbait?

"Do I get paid by the client?" I ask.

"They pay the agency, which takes its cut, and you get paid by the agency. Included in the paperwork is the W-9 tax form."

"How much is the agency's cut?"

"Twenty percent."

I have no idea if that's normal or not. On twenty thousand dollars, I would still get sixteen thousand, which is a mind-boggling amount for one night's work. Or less than that.

"What happens if, like, people find out?"

"What people? How would they find out?"

"I don't know. Just—could I get in trouble?"

"Look, Virginia, this is work. It's an acting gig. My agency rounds up the talent, if the talent is selected and booked, my agency gets paid, and the talent gets paid. Some acting gigs call for things like nudity. You've seen movies like *Basic Instinct* or *Showgirls*.

It's just like that."

The thought that I'm just an actor playing a part reassures me. A little. But maybe I'm just trying to find reasons to justify a bad idea.

I fill out the paperwork, which includes a lengthy nondisclosure agreement. I hesitate before signing. "What if I decide, at the last minute, that I can't go through with it?"

"Then you don't. But the NDA still stands—to protect everyone's privacy, you know. And of course you don't get paid. But I bet you could do a lot with twenty thousand extra dollars. Buy yourself some nice boots. Take a trip to Hawaii. Pamper yourself with a spa and shopping spree."

I look down at my pair of worn UGGs that I found at the Goodwill. They're a little big on me, but they were a steal. Maybe I could indulge in buying a pair of brand new UGGs that are actually my size.

After I finish the paperwork, Dan calls in the woman who had examined me and proceeds to notarize the NDA.

"I started out as a notary," he explains. He collects my thumbprint, then says, "You're all set, Virginia. Welcome aboard the Pullman Model and Talent Agency."

All of a sudden I feel like throwing up. I hurry out of the office and head to the restroom down the hall.

Just 'cause you signed some paper, doesn't mean you have to go through with it.

At a sink, I splash cold water onto my face.

It's a two-way street. The client has to like you, and you have to like him. Or at least find him tolerable.

But how could I find a man wanting to pay for sex with a virgin tolerable? And what if he's not gentle? Will he ruin sex for me?

I spend the rest of the day vacillating on my decision. I even think about asking Sierra what her experiences with Pullman have been. I stop by the hotel to see if Sierra is there and if they need extra staff. That's when I learn Mr. Lee has checked out. I find myself a little bummed. I wanted to get one more look at him—from a safe distance. I'm not sure why I find him intriguing even while he unsettles me. Maybe it's because he seems like he's from another place in time. Like he belongs in some 1930s gangster movie.

"She's preparing for some acting job," Tracy tells me when I ask about Sierra.

A few minutes later my cellphone rings. It's the Pullman Agency. With trembling hands, I take the call.

"Hey, Virginia," says Dan, "you got your first audition."

CHAPTER FIVE

"I can't take a week off from work on such short notice," I protest into the cellphone, hoping no one walks in on me in the break room. "I might lose my job. And it's the week before my econ midterm—"

"This client's willing to go twenty-five grand," Dan replies. "Clients like this don't come around every day."

"You said you had a model who got thirty thousand just last week."

"I don't usually get such high numbers back to back. Look, you interested in the pay or not? If not, I've got other talent I can send."

I put a hand to my brow. "I don't know. I thought this kind of thing was just a one-night deal."

"How many people you know make this much money in just one night?"

Silly me. I guess I don't know this business well.

"Is this twenty-five thousand for sure?" I ask.

"I won't let you work a job unless the pay is solid."

I can barely swallow. "I want a guarantee of some kind. Paid upfront."

"You don't get paid until I get paid."

"What happens if the client doesn't pay as promised?"

"That's what you've got me for. I go with all the talent to the auditions to make sure everything goes according to plan. If a talent is selected, the client has to pay fifty percent right then or he doesn't get the talent. Simple."

"How am I paid? Cash? Check?"

I realize I haven't thought through all the details. Checks could bounce. Cash could be counterfeit. And inconvenient. Only drug dealers would carry around that much cash, right?

"Once I have the down payment, I can deposit your cut into your bank account. Sheesh."

"Okay, let me think about it."

"You gotta let me know now. The audition's tomorrow. I'm driving all the talent up in the morning. You in or out?"

My pulse races. I hesitate, trying to think fast. Only my brain draws a blank.

"Okay," I blurt.

"Be at my office by eleven o'clock. And make sure you look your part."

"What's my part?"

But Dan has hung up.

I quiver on the inside. I can't believe I'm doing this. It all happened so fast. I thought I would get more time to sort out my buyer's remorse.

No need to get too worked up. I haven't even been

chosen.

I take a deep breath. I'll have to miss work tomorrow. If I don't get selected, it will have cost me a day's wages and study time. If I do get selected, well, I'll make more in a week than I would working months at the hotel. If I lose my job, I could find another.

And I can still bail, even after getting selected. Dan won't be happy, but if he thinks I can command that kind of money, he may not want to kick me to the curb, provided I'm still interested in trading in my virginity.

Feeling slightly better, I make it home. Sitting on my bed, I crack open my economics textbook, but there's no way I can study.

"Get changed. We're going to check out this new bar on Polk," Talia says as she enters the room.

"Actually, I think I'm going to stay in," I reply.

"You said you were going to go out with us tonight."

"I know, but I'm not feeling so hot right now."

It's not a lie. I don't feel good.

"You sure?"

I nod. "I might even skip studying and turn in early."

"All right. Hope you feel better."

I take a shower to calm my nerves, but I can't sleep, though I pretend to when I hear Talia and Alexia stumbling into the house around two in the morning. I'm a private person, and though I like my roommates a lot, I don't feel comfortable sharing what I'm up to. I can't think of anyone I would tell.

Eventually, I do fall asleep and wake up just before eight in the morning. Talia is in deep sleep and probably won't wake until noon. Quietly, I put on a camisole, sweater, and stretchy jeans. I'm not sure what "look the part" means, but I don't have anything fancy. I pack some clothes and toiletries in a duffel bag and head downstairs, where I call in sick. It's not a lie because I do feel nauseous.

Four other women, including Sierra, are waiting in the office when I arrive. They're dressed much nicer than I am. Two wear cocktail dresses. One wears a form-fitting sheath and four-inch heels. Sierra is in black leather leggings and a bustier that makes her ample breasts look even bigger.

She narrows her eyes at me. "What are *you* doing here?"

"Great recruit, Sierra," Dan says, walking up behind her. "If your friend gets selected, you'll qualify for a referral bonus."

She perks up. "How much?"

"If the pricing works out the way I think it will, five hundred."

She doesn't say anything to me after that.

Dan looks me over and wrinkles his face. "Not a fan," he says of my outfit, "but given your 'part,' it might actually work. At least put on some makeup."

Sierra snorts as she observes me applying some lip gloss and mascara, about the only makeup I own at the moment. The other women already have on the full range of cosmetics: foundation, powder, eye liner, lip liner, eye shadow, etc.

We pile into a van. I sit in the last row next to a beautiful Latina with perfect olive skin and super long eyelashes. I regret not thinking of making myself as presentable as possible, but I think it's because, deep down, I'm not fully committed to this.

"My name's Abril," she introduces.

I shake her hand, glad for any camaraderie in these unusual circumstances.

Sierra, sitting in front of me, turns around. "So you're a virgin, huh?"

"Yeah," I reply cautiously, wondering where she's going to take this.

"Kind of old to be a virgin, aren't you?"

I don't say anything. Her question is rhetorical anyway.

"How old are you?" asks a woman Dan had addressed earlier as Rachel. She seems to be in her mid-twenties and the oldest among us.

"Twenty-one," I respond.

"Wow. I lost my virginity when I was sixteen."

"I lost mine at fourteen," Sierra says.

"I'm nineteen and still a virgin," Abril says. "Is that old?"

"Hell yeah. You like super religious or

something?"

"I'm just Catholic."

"So why are you in this?"

"I think we're all here for the same reason, right?"

"Yeah, but I'm no fucking virgin. You really want this to be the way you pop your cherry?"

Abril flushes and looks down.

"Is a referral bonus always five hundred?" I ask in an innocent tone, but Sierra glares at me.

"I'm not really in it for the money," says Rachel. "I just want to meet rich men. No one else is worth having sex with."

"Seriously?" asks Julia, a petite Asian with large almond eyes. "What if he's totally ugly? What about a guy who doesn't have money but is totally ripped and hot?"

"I'd still take the rich guy. Money is the ultimate beauty."

"I'd take the hot guy," says Sierra. "'Course, the best would be a guy who's fucking rich *and* hot."

"Like that exists outside romance novels," scoffs Julia.

"Hot or rich doesn't make a guy good in bed," I offer.

"Listen to the virgin talk," Sierra sneers. "Like she would know anything about what it takes to be good in bed."

"What if a guy is rich and hot but a total jerk?" I ask of the other women.

"If that mattered, we wouldn't be here, would we?" Rachel returns.

"I bet the majority of men who are hot and rich are jerks," Julia muses. "I bet it gets to their heads."

"What the fuck are you talking about?" Dan interjects. "We're auditioning for a job, ladies, not some dating service. That's how you got to look at it."

"Who are we auditioning for?"

I see Dan's grin in the rearview mirror. "It's a surprise."

Abril has been quiet, so I ask where she lives. We converse a little about where our families are from and where we work—all safe subjects. Abril would like to enroll in community college but has to work to help her parents support five younger siblings and a grandmother.

Sierra doesn't bother with me the rest of the drive. Dan cranks up the radio. Rachel puts on Beats to listen to her own music. Julia falls asleep against the window.

An hour later, after winding up to the top of a hill with views overlooking the Pacific, the van pulls up in front of a stunning three-storied house guarded by several palm and cypress trees. My jaw drops at all the perfectly manicured plants, the floor-to-ceiling windows, and a deck that seems to wrap the entire house.

"Sweet," Rachel exhales as we get out.

A butler, or maybe he's some kind of security guard, opens the door, and we follow Dan into a large foyer with marble floors and a chandelier overhead. All of us except Dan gawk at our surroundings.

"You can take 'em into the den," the butler/guard tells Dan.

I bring up the end as we pass through the living room with panoramic views of the coastline and down several steps to a more rustic-looking room with oak panels, bookcases, the largest flat-screen TV I have ever seen, a billiard table, and a bar. Not just a counter with sink but an entire bar, like someone airlifted part of a restaurant into this room. Bottles of all shapes and colors line the shelves behind the mahogany bar, which has several stools pulled up to it.

A man about thirty years old sits on a large leather sofa with his arms spread across the back of it. With dark brown hair cut short, framing his brow in a rectangular shape, a rounded jawline that gives him a boyish look, and a small dent in his chin, he's good-looking save for the smug expression on his face. He looks clean cut and like someone Lila might approve of, though Lila would never judge a person just on their appearance. Nevertheless, I try to decide if he's someone I would be okay crawling into bed with.

My gaze travels to the far corner of the room,

where a cue rack is mounted—and my breath stops halfway up my windpipe.

CHAPTER SIX

In front of the rack, cue stick in hand, stands Tony Lee.

He recognizes me, and his face darkens.

Damn.

Even if I don't get selected and only miss one day of work, I'm out of a job for sure.

I want to look away, but his gaze traps mine.

"So what do you have for us today?" asks the man I now realize is Eric Drumm.

"Nothing but the best," Dan replies. "All good American stock, the way you like it. No Russian skanks or underage Thai girls."

Eric gets up to make a closer inspection of the women. He's much shorter than his dad, the governor of Florida, whom I've read is six and a half feet tall.

Having managed to tear my gaze from Mr. Lee, I look down at the hardwood flooring. My heart beats a mile a minute. Should I back out now? Or should I wait? Maybe I won't even get picked.

"What's with this one?" Eric asks of me.

My face turns beet red. I'm sure the color takes over my whole face. I don't blush pretty. Instead, I tend to look like fruit...cherries, apples, cranberries.

"She's special," Dan drawls. "The innocent girl-next-door you always wanted to bang and turn into a whore."

I think I look more like an eggplant now. I can't do this.

Eric looks at my chest. "Interesting, but I'm more of a tit-man." He walks over to Sierra and takes a long look at her cleavage. "This one looks real good."

Sierra gives him an encouraging smile.

"But I should let my guest pick first." He turns to look over at Lee. "See anything you like?"

"If not, I've got more back in the city," Dan adds. "Any color, shape you want."

"Only five thousand each for the week."

"Except the virgins. That would be the two lovely ladies at the end there. Mr. Drumm and I agreed their special qualities command a much higher price."

Lee stares at Eric with a frown. "I don't need to buy my women."

"I don't either," Eric replies, "but it's a lot more fun this way. Plus, they've been screened, and the NDAs are taken care of. Less hassle for us. No worries that some bitch might be trying to take secret pics of you to sell to the tabloids, though my dad's attorney has a great connect with most of them. And there are no expectations beyond the week. So which one do you like? You can pick two if you want. I know price isn't a concern for you."

"I'm paying?"

Eric looks slightly abashed. "I guess—as the host—it's my treat."

Even though the Drumms are worth something like three billion dollars, it's clear Eric isn't thrilled with having to pay. He walks over to Julia. "How about this one? She's cute."

"The one at the end."

I start. Is he referring to me?

"Great choice," Dan beams.

My pulse escalates. I panic, which shuts down my thinking. If I were facing a saber-tooth tiger, I'd be dead meat.

Eric leans over to Dan. "Did you say they were fifteen thousand?"

Dan looks taken aback. "We agreed twenty-five thousand, Mr. Drumm."

Eric purses his lip in displeasure. "Right. I guess I'll take the blond."

"Great choice," Dan repeats. "I'll be in touch with your assistant, Ms. Sanderson, about the particulars."

Eric nods. Dan begins to usher Rachel, Abril and Julia out. I want to follow them but am still frozen to my spot. Feeling Lee's gaze on me, I glance toward him. He doesn't look happy at all and turns to the billiard table, aiming the stick at the cue ball.

Eric walks over. "Why does this pool table look so

large?"

"This table isn't yours?" Lee asks.

"This isn't my place. It belongs to one of my dad's attorneys. I don't really like traveling to California. I mean, why come to this state when the sun in Florida is just as nice? Too many crazies and hippies live in this state."

"So why do you want to develop here?"

"Makes financial sense. That's what makes us Drumms such great businessmen. My dad's willing to stomach his distaste for this commie red state if the opportunity is right."

The men seem to have forgotten us, like we're maids back at The Montclair.

"So we supposed to keep standing here looking pretty for you boys?" Sierra pipes up.

Eric grins at her. He nods to the butler/guard. "Joe'll show you to your rooms."

Sierra returns a smile. Meanwhile, Lee doesn't look up at me. His cue ball strikes the red ball near the other end of the table.

I don't understand. Leering, ogling, pawing—I would have expected those behaviors. Lee seems disgruntled.

Sierra and I follow Joe up to the main floor and then up another flight of stairs to our respective bedrooms. Mine appears every bit as nice as a room in The Montclair. Patio doors lead to the deck that I saw from the front of the house. The queen bed has like a dozen pillows on it and faces a wide fireplace.

I never dreamed of actually sleeping in a room as nice as the ones I clean, but my circumstances prevent me from enjoying it. I think I would have been more at ease had I been chosen by Eric. I don't think I would have liked losing my virginity to him. There's something icky about him. And I think I would have come away with that feeling even if I had met him in a normal setting, like at a bar or grocery store. But Tony Lee...

Damn.

I sit on the edge of the bed, then leap to my feet.

Condoms! I forgot to get some. What if Lee doesn't have any? How would I get one? Would they let me make a run to the nearest drugstore? Then I realize if I spend the night, my roommates will worry about me.

Good going, I tell myself. I find my cellphone and think about what to tell them. I text Talia that I have to work late and might just spend the night at the hotel. I hope she believes me.

Sinking back down on the bed, I bury my head in my hands. I shouldn't go through with this. I'm not prepared. Plus, I'm not even sure Tony Lee likes me. You'd think he would, given that he chose me, but then why didn't he seem interested? He probably would have been just as excited to purchase insurance or one of those annoying additional warranties that the stores try to push onto all electronic gizmos. And because the cashier brings it up just as you're checking out, you wind up having to make a quick calculation to see if it's worth an extra twenty bucks to save yourself a hundred and fifty bucks on the off chance your printer breaks down in the next two or three years. Do I know the probability of a printer breaking down? Hell no.

Do I know the probability that this is all worth it for twenty thousand dollars?

Hell no.

CHAPTER SEVEN

From the bedroom window, I see Tony Lee, Eric Drumm and the man named Joe get into a car. I'm not sure where they're going, but their departure gives me more breathing room. I spend the next hour staring at the ceiling as I lay on the bed. The down comforter is amazingly soft, and I've never slept in a bed with down before, but I barely notice. My mind still turns. Maybe I should see how things go and pull the plug if I get really uncomfortable.

But I'm uncomfortable now.

I mean really, really uncomfortable. I wonder if there are any special exercises I should be doing down there to prepare myself. I've heard women mention Kegel exercises, but I think that had to do with postpartum stuff.

Despite my concerns, I find myself also wondering what Tony Lee would be like in bed. The year after graduating high school, I almost did it with a boy I was dating. I might have gone all the way, but he ended up ejaculating just from rubbing himself against me.

"Beginner's luck," scoffs Sierra from the doorway.

I sit up. "I'm not sure I can go through with this."

She narrows her eyes. "Are you stupid or something? You're going to pass up the opportunity to have sex with Tony Lee? I'd do him for free, but your redneck ass is going to get paid a buttload of money to do him."

"Just because I'm from North Carolina doesn't mean I'm a redneck."

"Whatever. I got nothing for losing my virginity."

"I think he knows I work at The Montclair. I still get paid for the hours I worked this week, even if I'm fired, right?"

Sierra rolls her eyes. "Why would he buy you if he wants to fire you?"

"I don't know. It's just the look he had on his face. I'm sure he's not happy that one of the hotel employees is...doing this."

She shrugs. "Well, maybe you're right."

"Have you...have you done this sort of gig before?"

"Only a few times. But it actually pays better than the modeling jobs I've gotten. And if Drumm gets elected president? How many women can say they've slept with the son of the frickin' president of the United States?"

"I signed an NDA that said I can't say *anything* about this. No who, what, where, when and why."

"Yeah, yeah. I signed that, too. Dan says it's to protect us as much as them."

"In what way?"

"I don't know. I don't really care as long as I get paid."

"And there's never a problem with getting paid?"

"You have to give Dan his cut, but other than that, it's easy money."

I want to ask her about her other experiences but don't want to exasperate her. I do have one pressing question, though.

"Are we supposed to provide the condoms or them?"

She does a double take. "You're not on birth control?"

"I tried birth control pills when I had really bad cramps as a teenager, but the pills gave me headaches."

"Sucks to be you. Guess you better hope Tony carries some."

She leaves me to stew in my quandary. Her bedroom is next to mine. I hear the sound of her cellphone camera and remember her showing Tracy modeling photos she took of herself for her Instagram account.

What am I going to do? What would Lila advise?

Not to get myself in such a mess in the first place.

Money isn't everything.

If you're going to jump, jump with two feet, otherwise you land crooked.

I realize I have one foot in, one foot out. Part of me wants to go through with it. Part of me wants to run the hell away. Maybe I need to keep my eyes on the prize. Twenty thousand dollars. Andre's football. Less stress for Lila. My future. Money may not be everything, but it was a means to some pretty important things.

And if I'm going to lose my virginity, why not get paid a buttload of money for it? I could hear the envy when Sierra spoke. Maybe I should consider myself lucky and be grateful for this opportunity. I could do far worse for my first sexual partner. Tony was good-looking. He was nice. Sort of.

Somehow I manage to drift asleep. When I wake, I realize I'm hugging one of the throw pillows, and I'm hungry. I never did get lunch. I look into Sierra's room and find that she's also napping. I go in search of the kitchen, hoping I don't come across anyone. If anyone works in this house and wonders who I am, I'm not sure what to tell them. Luckily, the house seems empty.

I couldn't even dream of living in a place like this. The living room ceiling is at least thirty feet high, the modern furniture is immaculate, and the hardwood floors gleam as if they were just installed yesterday. The kitchen is just as impressive. And huge.

Finding a fruit bowl, I help myself to an apple. Surely whoever can afford this place won't mind a missing apple.

I finish exploring the rest of the house except for

the upstairs. By the time I make it back to my room, I hear sounds of people entering the house. A few minutes later, Joe appears at my door and tells me to dress for dinner. I dig through the duffel bag that he had brought up earlier. What in the world do I wear?

If I want Tony Lee to change his mind about me, I should go with my sweats and my Michael Jordan Tarheels jersey. I had bought it for Andre for his twelfth birthday, but he grew out of it fast.

If I don't want Tony to change his mind...

I choose a dress I've worn to church before because it's actually the nicest thing I own, and put a sweater over it.

"Do all Southern girls have the same sense of fashion?" Sierra asks from the threshold. She's wearing a halter mini and thigh-high boots. Lila would never let me be caught dead wearing something like that, but a little bit of me is envious. I wish I had the guts to wear something like what Sierra has on. Not to care who might think it looked slutty.

"Not everyone's as lucky as you," I reply with sincerity, slipping on a pair of strappy sandals I bought when my roommates and I went outlet shopping, and then reapplying some makeup. "I don't have a body that could pull off a dress like yours."

Mollified, Sierra makes no further comment. We

head downstairs and find the men in the dining room having drinks at the bar. Sierra sidles up to Eric as if they've been dating for a long time.

She indicates the tequila he's having. "I'll take one of those. With a twist of lime."

Eric makes her drink. "Let me know if you want seconds."

I look at the shot glass Tony holds. It looks like some kind of whiskey. I could use a drink to calm my nerves. Eric is busy grinning at Sierra, so that leaves Tony to attend to me.

"Are you old enough to drink?" he asks.

"I'm twenty-one, but I'll start with water," I say. Maybe I'll have a glass of wine with dinner."

Tony opens a glass bottle and pours a cup of water for me.

"Thanks," I say. I still can't tell what he thinks of me. I know he's taken me in with one look of those dark eyes of his, and I find myself wishing I could look half as hot as Sierra. Or half as hot as him. His hair has less gel this time around, and he has on relaxed slacks and a lightweight sweater that shows off his broad shoulders and pecs.

"What's your name?" he asks me.

It's an obligatory question, one a drill sergeant might ask a new recruit.

"Virginia."

He tries the name. "Virginia. Like the state?"

"Good Southern name, my mom says."

He doesn't say anything more. Next to us, Eric has wrapped his arm around Sierra. Tony and I stand at a stiff distance from each other.

I try to make polite conversation. "I'm not from Virginia, though. I'm from North Carolina. Tarheel state."

He only stares at me. Assessing me.

I try harder. "You ever been there?"

"No. I've never traveled to the Southern United States."

Glad to have a response from him, I continue, "Oh, it's pretty. I miss the autumn colors especially. The seasons aren't as distinct in California, though I'm not complaining as the weather is nice here. Do you come here, to California, often?"

"At least two to three times a year."

Silence follows.

Luckily for me, dinner is served. I don't know where the server came from. Does she live in the house or just work during the day?

We sit down at a table that seats twelve. Eric sits at the head of the table, Lee is to his right, and Sierra to his left. I decide to sit next to Sierra instead of Lee. The server starts us off with something called an aperitif. The appetizer is something called a tartare served in a glass garnished with capers and lime.

"This is like being in a fancy restaurant," says Sierra as she finishes off the aperitif. "Do you eat like this every night?"

"Nah," Eric replies. "My favorite food is good old American fare, pizza, hot dogs, hamburgers—with good homegrown beef. Not that fancy Kobe beef."

"I thought pizza is Italian," Sierra giggled.

"Pizza in Italy is nothing like what we have here. There's barely any cheese or toppings there. Americans have improved on it. The best things in life are either invented by Americans or improved by us."

Lee raises a brow. "You drive an Audi."

Eric bristles.

"And half the wines in your bar are French," Lee adds.

"We're catching up to the Frenchies on wine. Napa wines have kicked French ass. Before long, Florida wines will be up there with them. My father owns two wineries, one in Tampa and another in St. Augustine. Your family ever think about going into the wine business? It's the fashionable thing to do. Everyone's got to have their own label."

"We have a joint enterprise with D'Argent in Xinjian."

"Man, I'd love to sell some of our wines over in China."

Lee seems amused. "But your father is advocating more tariffs on Chinese imports. That's not the best way to encourage China to welcome American goods."

"That's just to correct the trade imbalance. It's not fair that we buy more from China than you do from us."

"What's capitalism without a free economy? We're just giving the American consumer what they want. And if you're able to produce more of what the Chinese want, they'll happily buy from you."

"Tariffs can actually backfire and do the opposite of increasing exports to China," I parrot what my economics instructor, Mr. Parker, once said. "If other countries produce the same thing, China may start to buy from them. Once they get in the habit of doing so, they may not come back."

Everyone stares at me. From the look on Sierra's face, I must have bugs crawling out of my head. Eric looks dumbfounded. And Tony Lee...again, I can't quite tell what he's thinking. The guy should become a professional poker player.

"What, you go to business school or something?" Eric asks. From the derision in his tone, I gather it's a rhetorical question.

"We just started the topic of international trade in my economics class," I reply. I suppose it is absurd for me to offer up anything in the company of men who know a helluva lot more about business and the economy than me.

"That's quaint." Eric looks to Tony. "My dad believes in the tough love approach. He's not going to be a wuss like our opponent."

"What is this?" Sierra asks as she pokes at the second appetizer, seared scallop on a bed of risotto, which I think is some kind of rice, and drizzled with pesto.

"You never had scallops before?"

She scrunches her face and pushes the plate away. "I'm not a fan of seafood. But I'll take another shot of tequila."

I've never had scallops before but give it a try.

O.M.G.

I never knew a piece of meat could be so *buttery*. It's actually more amazing than lobster to me. Or maybe it's cause I've never had lobster prepared like this. And the rice thing beneath the scallop is so rich and creamy, making the dish otherworldly.

In my gastric euphoria, I must look like a fool because Lee is staring at me.

"It's really good," I explain and quickly busy myself with my plate. I wish he'd stop staring at me like that.

The main course is something I'm more familiar with—filet mignon. Not that I've had a lot of filet mignon in my life, but my adoptive father, Maurice—or "Mo"—was a pretty mean griller. I'd actually take his ribs, smothered in his homemade rub, over just about anything.

I drink some of the red wine that's paired with the steak. I'm guessing it's a really good wine, but I can't tell the difference and it's a little too peppery for my taste.

Since the topic of trade had turned a little too political for comfort, the talk turned to safer topics like travel.

"That resort your family developed in Con Dao is pretty sweet," Eric remarks. He looks startled, then smiles over at Sierra. I suspect she's playing footsies under the table.

"Different part of the family. My father's cousin."

"Would that be the father of Benjamin Lee?"

"Yes."

"How close are you to the mafia Lees?"

Wine in hand, Tony sits back in his chair. "What are you talking about?"

Eric's arm subtlety moves up and down, like he's stroking a pet dog beneath the table. He leans in toward Tony.

"My father's oppo team did some investigating. Got to make sure we know who we're dealing with in business."

"What is an 'oppo team'?"

"Opposition research. Every campaign, especially presidential campaigns, run opposition research. We do it in business, too. So you pretty tight with the Chinese mafia?"

"You worry about us? You might want to look at some of your existing business partners."

There's something left unsaid, but I'm not sure what it is.

Eric gives a nervous laugh and looks over at Sierra. "You want dessert?"

"Of course," Sierra purrs.

Like the scallops over risotto, dessert—a flourless chocolate torte topped with some kind of French cream—is to die for. I didn't think my stomach had room for more food but I manage to eat every last bite. I feel Tony's gaze again and glance up. Sure enough, he's observing me. Blatantly.

The champagne served with wine is more my style, and I drink that up. Hopefully it will ease my nerves because dinner is over, and that means we're closer to what I came and auditioned for.

CHAPTER EIGHT

"More tequila?" Eric asks Sierra after we've gone downstairs to the den.

"Let's change it up," Sierra replies. "How about Sex on the Beach?"

Eric grins. "A staple from my days at U Penn."

He and Sierra head to the bar. I stall at the threshold, not sure where to plant myself.

Tony indicates the sofa. "Sit."

I'm glad to have a destination.

"What about you, Tony? There's even some *baijiu* if you want."

"I'll try that Springbank scotch," Tony replies as he takes a seat on the other side of the sofa from me.

"You want a chaser with that?"

"You have a lime seltzer?"

"Yep."

To avoid Tony's gaze, I look out the window at the gorgeous view with the grayish waters of the Pacific rolling toward shore.

"How 'bout you—Virginia, is it?"

"Um...I don't know..."

Lila and Mo never had alcohol at home. In high school, the kids that drank gravitated towards Bud or Coors.

"I can whip you up a Long Island Iced Tea."

"Sure..."

"Don't overdo it," Tony warns Eric.

"Ahh," Eric groans. "That takes the fun out of the drink."

After handing everyone their drinks, Eric plops down on a large leather armchair and pulls Sierra onto his lap.

"You ladies having fun yet?" he asks.

"Omigod, yes," Sierra replies. "Who wouldn't be? You've got like every drink in existence here and a badass chef. Does he work just for you?"

"He came with the house."

"This house is fuckin' amazing. I would kill to live in a place like this. You own a house like this?"

"My family owns several. Even bigger and badder. In Florida, where the beaches are much warmer. Northern California beaches aren't like real beaches. They're fucking freezing most of the time."

She twirls a finger into his hair. "You own houses in Hawaii, too? That would be my beach of choice."

"Yeah, we've got a place on Maui." Eric nods toward Tony. "How many places does your family own?"

Tony gives a small grin. "Is that some kind of proxy for dick size?"

I can't help but chuckle and end up coughing on my drink, which is actually quite tasty.

"Drink it slow," Tony tells me. "You can't taste it, but there's a lot of alcohol in a Long Island Iced Tea."

"I'm telling you, you'll thank me later," Eric says as he rubs Sierra's lower back. "So you really a model?"

Sierra nods and nestles farther against him.

"My last girlfriend was a lingerie model. Super high maintenance. Always on a different diet. Drove me fuckin' crazy with it. I couldn't eat a burger without her talking about carbs and shit."

"I love hamburgers."

He had a few of his buttons undone on his shirt, and she swirled a finger in the opening where his chest hairs were visible.

"Yeah? What else do you love?"

They seemed to have forgotten Tony and I were still there. I take another sip of my drink.

After a long minute, he reaches for the box on the coffee table and offers me a cigar. "Would you like one?"

I shake my head. Although North Carolina is known for its tobacco, I'm not a smoker.

"Mind if I smoke?"

I do, but I'm just a guest. Maybe not even that. I'm a purchase. So I shake my head and watch him light the end of a cigar.

Eric looked up. "If you like cigars, I'll send you a box of Arturo Fuente. See how you like 'em. They're

Florida-based."

Sierra slides her hand under his shirt, drawing his attention. I clear my throat. It's clear she and Eric are going to be getting it on. How in the world do I start with Tony? Should I try to get it over with sooner rather than later? Is he expecting I'll make the first move?

I study how his middle finger curves under the cigar, and how his forefinger rests over the top of it to keep it in place. He has masculine hands, I decide. But there's a certain grace to the way he holds the cigar.

Maybe I should try to get to know him a little better? Get him to like me? Then again, he chose me so quickly out of all the women, he can't *not* like me, right?

"Is Virginia your real name?" he asks after a silence that seemed to last forever but doesn't seem to bother him.

"Yes," I reply, not sure if it's a good sign or not that he's asking me questions.

"What's your last name?"

I consider giving a fake name, but he could easily access the hotel payroll to get my full name, birthdate, and social.

"Mayhew. Actually, it's Mayhew-Porter. Mayhew's my biological mother's name. Porter is my adoptive family's name."

"You have an accent."

"I haven't been in California that long. Born and lived most of my life in North Carolina. You ever been to the Carolinas?"

I recall that he already said he's never been to the South.

"We're not all rednecks," I blurt, then wonder why the hell I said that.

"What is a 'red-neck'?"

"It's a derogatory term for a white person from the South who's not very, um, cultured, and who's often a bigot. What part of China are you from?"

"I'm not from China. I spend far more time in Vietnam than China."

"You're Vietnamese?"

"I'm Chinese, but my family settled in Vietnam hundreds of years ago."

"Your English is very good," I say, then wish I hadn't in case he might take offense at that. I sip more of my drink.

"It's okay. My French is better."

"You speak French, too?"

"Vietnam was a French colony until the 1950s. Many families of privilege sent their children to Paris to be educated. My family temporarily moved to Paris after the war. I was born there."

"Did you grow up there?"

"Mostly."

"I'd love to go to Paris someday. My family didn't travel a lot, not even to popular destinations within

North Carolina like the Smokey Mountains or Nags Head. Did you like it in Paris?"

He draws on the cigar and releases the smoke in one long breath. "It's worth visiting."

That seems like an understatement for a city considered among the most beautiful in the world. "Are there places you like better?"

"No. They're just different."

We're back to silence. I end up finishing my drink. I would continue the conversation, but I'm not sure he's all that interested.

"We're gonna hit the hot tub," Eric announces. "Want to join?"

"I didn't bring a swimsuit," I reply.

"Who says you need to wear a suit?"

Sierra has started to unbutton the rest of his shirt. Eric looks over at Tony.

"I'll pass."

I'm a little relieved. If he went, I would probably be obligated to go, too.

Eric and Sierra remove various articles of clothing on their way to the hot tub, which is out on the deck. I hear Sierra giggling. The sliding glass door opens, then closes.

I'm alone with Tony.

CHAPTER NINE

My heart throbs with each beat. Here it is. The moment. It's imminent. Now would be a good time to bail. I could probably catch a taxi home if needed.

I half expect him to slide over to my side of the sofa, but he seems content where he is as he finishes his cigar. My head has started to swim a little from the alcohol I've consumed. I don't think I can take the suspense anymore. I need to make a decision once and for all about this.

"So, um," I start when he doesn't say or do anything. "I've never really done this before."

He turns his dark eyes to me. "That's obvious."

"It is?"

"You wouldn't be a virgin otherwise."

God, I'm dumber than a box of rocks. Maybe alcohol really does kill brain cells.

He puts out his cigar and stands up, walks to the bar and comes back with a glass of water. "Drink it. It will help with the hangover."

"I'm getting a hangover?"

"You had two glasses of champagne, a Long Island Iced Tea, and you look like you barely weigh over a hundred."

I drink the water. Can I mess this up further?

"Where are your parents?"

He asks as if I'm a teenager hanging out after curfew.

"My adoptive father passed away when I was twelve, and my mother's in North Carolina. My adoptive mother, that is. My birth mother lives in San Mateo."

"Do they know what you're doing?"

I flush. "I only met my birth mother six months ago, and...she's not really that interested in me. And Lila, no, she doesn't know."

He watches me drink the water. When I finish, he takes the glass from me.

"You should go to bed. Try to sleep off the vodka and gin."

"There's vodka *and* gin in what I drank?"

"And rum."

No wonder I feel like I'm halfway to being Cooter Brown. It feels good, but I get the feeling I'm going to pay for it later.

"I had no idea," I half say to myself. I look up at him. Is he serious about letting me go to bed?

He stares at me for several intense seconds, then returns the glass to the bar. "Go."

I stand up, and the room immediately wavers. I right myself. "Really? What about...?"

He waits for me to finish my sentence, but surely

he knows what I'm referring to?

"You just want me to go to sleep?" I query. "That's it?"

"I expect employees to follow their directives."

But I'm not— Is he referring to me as a hotel employee or a different kind of employee?

"Does anyone else at the hotel, other than Sierra, know what you do or facilitate this in any way?" he asks.

"No! No, this was totally spur of the moment. Even Sierra didn't know I was..."

Part of me wants to beg him not to fire me. It's not that I like being a hotel maid so much, but I don't want to have to go job hunting with midterms coming up.

I should beg him to let me keep my job.

That might come across too desperate.

I don't need the hotel job. I'm going to get paid twenty thousand dollars.

Oh, right.

But that's only if I go through with it.

"Come on," he says, returning and taking my elbow. His grasp is firm but a touch gentle. It's probably the alcohol, but I feel like melting into him.

"What are you doing?" I ask warily as he guides me toward the double doors.

"I'm going to make sure you don't fall down the stairs."

"I don't think I would—"

I stumble, and he catches me with both hands to steady me.

"I'm just naturally klutzy," I mumble.

Why do his hands feel so good on me?

He walks me up to the third floor to my room. His is down the hall facing the ocean.

"Next time you might want to skip the Long Island Iced Tea," he says, sitting me on the bed.

I nod in agreement as the room wavers more than ever. I watch him go down on one knee to slip off my sandals. My pulse skips as his fingers brush against me.

He rises. "Do you have night clothes you want to change into?"

"Um, I've got a T-shirt. It's in my bag."

He spots my duffel bag and goes over to find the shirt. He comes back with a faded light blue Carolina shirt. It's old and the seams are coming out, but it's comfortable because it's worn. He sets it on the bed next to me. I stare at it. So he's really not expecting anything tonight?

"What's the matter?" he asks. "You need help getting undressed?"

My mind is still pondering my own question, and he interprets my non-answer as an affirmative to his question. He takes a knee on the bed behind me and gently pulls down the zipper of my dress. I can feel the air on my back and the faintest of heat from his body. With a difficult swallow, I slip my arms out of my dress and pull the shirt over me. I feel his weight come off the bed, and I maneuver my bra off underneath my shirt, before sliding the rest of my dress off.

By now, Tony has gone into the bathroom and returned with a cup of water. My shirt isn't that long and comes down to my upper thighs, and he seems to glance briefly at my bare legs. I feel practically naked in front of him.

"Drink," he directs.

I do as he says. Honestly, I can't imagine not doing what he tells me. I'm probably going to have to go to the bathroom half a dozen times tonight.

He pulls down the covers and nods for me to get in. He's putting me to bed. I guess he doesn't want to do it with a drunk girl. Maybe he's worried that I'll throw up on him.

After I crawl into bed, he pulls the covers over me. I watch him turn off the lights and close the door behind him as he leaves. No good night. Nada.

I lie in darkness, confused, a mixture of relief and concern. So what am I supposed to do now?

CHAPTER TEN

Because I hadn't shut the blinds, light streams in, filling the bedroom. I block out the brightness by burying my head beneath a pillow. I have a headache, but the hangover could be worse. After lying in bed for several minutes without being able to sleep, I peek out from beneath the pillow and try to remember what happened last night.

Nothing. Nothing happened.

And part of me is disappointed. If I haven't fulfilled my job, does it mean I won't get paid? This concerns me. If I'm not going to get paid, I don't want to lose my job at The Montclair.

The Montclair! What time is it?

I throw the covers aside and, stumbling out of bed, am rewarded with a throb of the head. I fumble for my cellphone. 10:48! I was supposed to be at work over an hour ago! With shaky hands, I quickly dial the hotel.

"Mrs. Ruiz," I greet when the operator transfers me. "I am so, so sorry. I meant to call earlier that I can't make it in today."

"I know," she responds.

"You...?"

"I saw the note when I came in this morning that you weren't coming in. You're not feeling well?"

"I'm not feeling well," I confirm, puzzled.

"We have a wedding party coming in at the end of the week. Hopefully you'll be better by then?"

"I—I hope so."

After hanging up, I head to Sierra's room. Maybe she called the hotel. But Sierra's bed doesn't look like it's been slept in.

Back in my own room, I brush my teeth, remember Tony's point to stay hydrated and drink two cups of water, and decide to run a bath. The bathroom Talia and I share only has a shower, so a bath is a rare treat. This tub even has jets. I snuggle into the hot water and consider what I'm going to do with myself.

Except for staring at my legs for a few seconds, Tony hadn't shown any real interest in doing anything with me last night. Was I that unappealing? But then why did he choose me in the first place? Was it because I was drunk? Is he shy himself? That seems implausible. He seems the kind of man who knows what he wants it, goes after it, and gets it.

If he has buyer's remorse and decided he doesn't want me anymore, then nothing gained, nothing lost. I should just get myself back home as soon as possible so I don't miss any more days of work or class.

If he still wants to...do I still want to as well?

The answer comes back even stronger than before: yes.

Yesterday I had reasoned that I should jump in with both feet. I had recounted all the benefits of making twenty thousand dollars. And while he still makes me a little uneasy, I'm also drawn to him. Given how my body came to life at his touch, I can't deny it. I wasn't fully ready to go all the way last night, but I had wanted him to stay.

I envy Sierra her lack of timidity. Maybe that's another plus that Talia alluded to when she talked about getting virginity out of the way. After you lose it, you can relax.

After the bath, I drink another cup of water and try to make myself as presentable as possible. I wear my skinny jeans and a black camisole. I consider wearing a sweater but decide against it. I blow-dry my hair, which I don't usually do unless I have to, and apply my lip gloss and mascara. By the time I'm done, my headache has settled into a dull instead of throbbing ache.

My stomach growls, and I head downstairs in search of breakfast. The house seems empty again, but I come across a maid in the kitchen.

"Good morning," I greet.

She looks up from wiping the counter to give me a quick smile before returning quietly to her work.

Like me at The Montclair, we're just ghosts moving in the background.

"I'm Virginia."

"Luciana," she replies with a heavy accent.

"Do you think anyone would mind if I help myself to a banana and a glass of milk?"

She looks confused.

"I'm just a guest," I explain.

"I think okay?"

I get the banana and milk, not wanting to cook without the host's permission or mess up the kitchen while it's being cleaned. My usual breakfast isn't fancy anyway, consisting mostly of a bowl of cereal and coffee. I miss Lila's grits.

After eating, I wander into the living room and stare out the windows at the view. A gorgeous, cloudless sky of blue stretches from the hills of Marin County to the city skyline. California has more than its fair share of days like this, I marvel.

I make my way down to the den where I remember seeing bookshelves. The clothes Sierra and Eric removed last night, including Sierra's bra and panties and Eric's boxers, are neatly folded on the sofa. Probably Luciana's doing. I wonder if she's had to pick up and fold a lot of underwear in her line of work. I've come across the occasional forgotten clothing item at the hotel, but we usually just toss it unless we think it's something the guest will contact the hotel to get back.

I browse the books on the shelves. I would have brought my econ textbook, but I think I left it in class. Many of the books before me seem to be biographies of famous golf players, how-to books on improving one's golf swing, and reviews of the world's best courses. There are a few biographies of famous football coaches and quarterbacks as well as biographies of American businessmen, from Henry Ford to Lee Iacocca to Elon Musk. I pick out a book that looks older than the rest: *Think and Grow Rich* by Napoleon Hill. If only it were that easy.

Book in hand, I head back upstairs and find Sierra in the kitchen. Wearing only a satin robe, she peruses the refrigerator and finds leftovers from last night's dinner.

"Ugh, I could really use some Starbucks right now," she groans as she takes out a plate of the chocolate torte from last night. "Where did they go anyway?"

I shrug my shoulders. I could use some coffee, too, but I don't see a coffeemaker, only a fancy espresso machine I have no idea how to operate. But I do find a kettle and a container of loose tea leaves and dried flower petals. It's interesting because I've only ever had tea from bags.

"Want some tea?" I ask as I fill the kettle with water and put it on the stove.

Sierra scrunches up her face. "Gross." She digs into the torte. "So how was Tony Lee? He make you bleed a lot?"

My face grows warm. "He let me sleep. He didn't want to do anything."

"What? What a weirdo."

"I had a little too much to drink. I guess he was being nice about it."

"You honestly think that?"

"Or maybe he lost interest."

That seemed a more plausible reason to Sierra. "So you're still a virgin. Hunh. Can't even give it away?"

I let it go. It's not worth it.

"Thanks for calling the hotel," I offer.

"What are you talking about? I didn't call anyone."

Deciding further conversation with Sierra probably isn't worth the effort, I open the Napoleon Hill book. She finishes her dessert and, deciding the same about conversation, shuffles out of the kitchen and back upstairs. I make my tea and drink half of it. It turned out bland because I wasn't sure how much of the tea leaves to use.

Unable to focus on the book, I get my sweater and decide to wander around the outside of the house. There's a narrow dirt path that leads to stairs down to the beach. I can't imagine how much a house with access to the beach in the San Francisco Bay Area would cost. Several million at least. Maybe tens of million. Rent in the city is like three times what I'm used to seeing back in North Carolina.

The beach isn't very large and more rocky than sandy for most of it, but it's a beach, and it's beautiful. I close my eyes to better drink in the sound of waves crashing, transporting me away from my circumstances, away from my discontent.

Feeling a change in the air, I open my eyes. Tony Lee stands next to me, looking out at the ocean. He has on his trench coat, open in front to reveal the charcoal-colored three-piece suit he's wearing. I don't see many men in three-piece suits anymore, but he looks super stylish in his.

"There's lunch back at the house," he informs me after several minutes of silence.

"Thanks," I reply.

"How's the hangover?"

"Barely there. I think staying hydrated helped."

We fall back into silence, and I'm more at ease with it than I expect. I almost like it, enjoying his presence without having to talk or hope I don't say something stupid. But then I remember something.

"Did you call The Montclair?"

He looks at me.

"About me," I continue.

"I said you weren't coming in today."

"Thank you...just today?"

He appraises me before saying, "I'm sending you back."

To my surprise, I feel dismayed. "You're—but—

why?"

He pulls out a silver cigarette case from his coat and lights a cigarette. After inhaling, then exhaling, he turns back to me. "You don't know what you're doing."

Taken aback, I don't know what to say at first. "Excuse me?"

"I understand that you want the money, but this is not something you can undo. If you get buyer's remorse, there are no returns."

"I know that," I say quietly.

"Why do you need the money so badly?"

"Well, I don't make much of it at The Montclair. Lila—my mother—doesn't make much either back in North Carolina. And my younger brother, he's got a chance of getting a basketball scholarship, or so his coach says, if he can attend this special camp. Plus...there's a lot of good reasons."

"What about your biological father?"

"I don't know who my biological father is."

He taps the cigarette to dislodge the ashes before taking another draw. "A lot of people have things they need to pay for without resorting to what you're doing."

Finding his statement patronizing, I can't help replying, "Easy for someone like you to say."

He glances sharply at me.

Undaunted this time, I continue, "I have an opportunity, a unique opportunity, to make more money than I could working an entire year—well, I guess it would be more like two years because I only work part time because of school."

"Where do you attend school?"

"I'm taking classes at the community college, but I'm hoping to transfer to UC Berkeley in the fall."

His expression seems to soften—a little.

"Maybe you don't understand what a relief it would be not to have to worry about money for a change."

"I don't," he concedes. "My family always had money. At least since the fifteenth century on my mother's side of the family, when China took over Vietnam."

"That's a long time."

"You go through with your plan, the hangover is going to be worse than what you felt this morning."

"You don't know that."

He gives me a who-you-trying-to-kid look.

"Really," I say. "I'm very practical."

He doesn't seem to believe me. "Women always remember their first time."

"And men don't? Did you have a 'hangover' after yours?"

His stare deepens, and a faint smile tugs at a corner of his mouth. I realize how full his lips are. Usually I don't notice men's lips, almost as if they don't have any, but Tony's lips are supple and...sensuous.

"I do remember my first time," he says, his tone lighter than before. "I don't remember her name, but I remember what she looked like. And I remember it was hellishly humid because it was summer in Vietnam."

"And did you have buyer's remorse?"

"It's not the same for men."

I suppose that's true. Expectations for women around sex have changed but are still different. A wind has picked up, so I cross my arms in front of me.

"I'm willing to take the chance," I tell him. "I'm okay with the 'hangover.'"

"You say that now because you don't know how you will actually feel afterward."

I let out a breath, feeling like a child talking to her parent. It's true that I wasn't sure I wanted to go through with it yesterday because I didn't want to regret it later, but I want to be the one to make that decision, not have it made for me.

I rub my arms. He takes a last draw of his cigarette, then drops it into the sand before removing his coat and putting it around my shoulders. I reach up to pull the coat tighter about me and end up grazing his hand. His breath seems to stall. Mine does for sure.

I make up my mind then and there.

I want to do this.

CHAPTER ELEVEN

It takes me a few minutes to work up the guts to ask, "Why did you pick me if you didn't want...if you didn't want to do anything?"

He puts his hands in his pockets and gazes out at the ocean. I hang on to his silence, eager yet anxious for his reply.

He murmurs more to himself than me. *"Je sais pais."*

I've heard those words before, like in a movie, but can't remember what they mean. I bite down on my lower lip. If he sends me back, does that mean I don't get paid?

"Let's go inside," he says, turning toward the house.

His coat is heavy, but it protects me from the cold breeze. I bend down and pick up his discarded cigarette butt.

"What are you doing?" he asks.

"Picking up the litter," I reply.

He lets me go up the stairs first and follows me back into the house. Once inside, I thank him for the coat as I return it to him.

"Have lunch, then collect your things," he

instructs.

I walk into the kitchen to find Sierra, still in her satin robe, sitting at the island counter finishing off a sandwich. There are several other sandwiches and salads to choose from.

"What's the matter with you?" she asks when I poke at a salad without taking a bite.

"Tony's taking me back to the city," I reply.

"Why's that?"

"Guess he changed his mind about me."

She sips her Arnold Palmer through a straw. "Too bad. Would have been cool to lose your virginity to someone like Tony Lee. And make twenty thousand for it."

"I guess I blew it," I sigh.

She concurs. "Sucks to be you."

I give up on the salad and head upstairs to gather my things. Maybe if I hadn't been so indecisive yesterday...but he hadn't seemed inclined to want to do anything anyway.

With my duffel bag in hand, I descend the stairs and can hear voices from the foyer.

"Where you going?" Eric asks.

"I'm taking Virginia back to the city," Tony replies.

"Yeah? She no good?"

No response.

"Does she not suck dick?" Eric clarifies. "Does her cunt smell bad?"

"I wouldn't know. I put her to bed."

"What? Why? I mean, she's maybe a six or seven out of ten, eight if she had some style, but that's not bad. If she's not pretty enough for you—"

"She's pretty," he says firmly.

"You decide you can't bang a virgin then? I can take care of that if you want."

No response again. I hear the sound of keys.

"Well, if you take her back, make sure Dan knows I'm not paying. Maybe you can trade her in for one of those other girls."

Not wanting to hear more of how I might get exchanged like a defunct product being taken back to the store, I descend the stairs and enter the foyer where Tony is waiting. He's changed into more casual slacks, a sport shirt, and a dark leather jacket. He puts on his sunglasses. He looks devastatingly sexy.

Damn. I messed up big time.

I follow him outside and get into a black sports car of some kind. He puts my duffel bag in the trunk before opening the passenger door for me. I climb into soft leather seats.

He starts to drive, and we make our way down the winding road that takes us into town. We're almost at Highway 101 when I finally work up the courage to say, "I don't want to go back to the city."

He doesn't respond and takes the car up the on-ramp.

"I'm serious," I say. "I've thought about it a lot, and I want to do this."

Still no response. We're on the freeway.

"I need the money," I add, "and losing my virginity is not going to be that big a deal."

He stares straight ahead. "You don't want to do it with me."

"Why not?"

"I have...preferences."

"Like what? Blonds? Asians? Non-virgins? Women with bigger boobs?"

He draws in a breath. "You know that book you are reading? *Fifty Shades*."

"Yeah?"

He turns to stare me. "Child's play."

I can't swallow. So he's into...BDSM. No biggie. I know about that now. Not like firsthand experience "know," but it's not something that I'm scared of. I don't think.

"That's okay," I reply.

He raises his brows.

"I'm open to trying new things," I insist.

He shakes his head.

"You keep thinking you know what I want or should want. I'm not this naive, can't-tie-my-own-shoes—"

"You're too young."

"I'm twenty-one, not sixteen or seventeen."

"I'm too old."

"How old are you?"

"Twenty-nine."

"Okay, that's old."

My answer surprises him, and he looks at me. Realizing I'm not serious, he lets out a chuckle. I like the sound of it.

"Any other objections?" I press.

"Yes. You're correct. I prefer blonds or Asians. And non-virgins."

I look down in disappointment, then up in puzzlement. Remembering I didn't get a satisfactory answer earlier, I ask, "Then why did you pick me yesterday?"

"I was being nice."

Oh. Guess I shouldn't have asked. I purse my lips, then say softly, "I'd rather you not be nice."

The muscle along his jaw tenses as he shifts into a higher gear so that we're driving beyond the speed limit, like he's in a hurry.

Feeling like I have nothing to lose at this point, I say, "Why do you care how I lose my virginity anyway? If I don't lose it to you, it'd probably be to some half-drunk frat boy whose name I won't care to remember."

He weaves between two cars so that he can get ahead of a car that's only doing seventy-five in the fast lane.

"You'd be doing me a favor," I try. "The money means a lot. And I don't know that I can work two jobs while studying at Berkeley. There are so many smart people at that school. Honestly, I don't know how I got in. I keep thinking there's another Virginia Mayhew out there who got the rejection letter I was supposed to get."

After a few minutes of silence, he says, "I'll give you the money."

My jaw drops. Is he being serious?

Incredulous, I inquire, "For what?"

"For Berkeley. For whatever you need it for."

He sounds a little frustrated. At first, I think he's like Eric, whom I suspect is a scrooge when it doesn't involve self-indulgence. But my intuition tells me Tony's different.

"So you're giving me, like, a scholarship?"

"Sure."

"And you're still taking me home?"

"Yes."

"That's...very philanthropic of you." I knit my brows. I should be ecstatic. Instead, I feel unsettled. "I'm sorry I'm not a blond or Asian non-virgin."

I watch his nostrils flair. He hasn't looked at me for a while. We sit in silence, which I'm almost used to by now. I tell myself I should keep my trap shut. It's like I hit the lotto. It doesn't feel real.

"You know, it's okay," I decide, even as a part of me is screaming that I'm a card short of a full deck. "You don't have to do that. You don't have to give me the money."

Now he turns to look at me, and even with his sunglasses on, I can see his disbelief.

"I know I said a lot about how important the money is, but...it's not your problem."

"Are you refusing my generosity?"

No.

Yes.

Because I'm crazy.

And an idiot.

"I wasn't looking to guilt you into charity."

"You wanted the money badly enough to give up your virginity, but now you won't take it because I won't have sex with you?"

It sounds ludicrous because it is. I don't know what I'm doing.

"So have sex with me," I say.

He blinks several times. His grip on the steering wheel tightens. He mutters something in French.

I realize I've upset him. On top of making no sense. I look out the window to my right and wish I was back at my apartment, so I can put this whole thing behind me.

Abruptly, he swerves the car all the way to the slow lane and pulls up on the shoulder. He puts the car in park and turns to me. I feel like withering beneath his stare.

"You won't take money unless I fuck you?" he demands.

I guess that's what I'm saying. It's hard to think

straight when he's looking at me like that, even with the sunglasses shading the flash in his eyes. For almost the entire time I've been in his company, he's been nothing but cool and collected. Occasionally, I would see a flair of emotion from beneath half-lidded eyes, but his tone was always calm. Till now.

"You could, um, not fuck me and not give me the money if you want," I offer.

He rolls his eyes once with a shake of the head. "I told you what my preferences are. I warned you."

I nod.

"*Putain de merde,*" he mutters.

He works the gearshift and pulls the car back onto the freeway. So what did he just decide? I almost dare not ask, but he speaks first.

"So where do you want to do it?"

Does this mean he's agreeing to have sex?

When I don't answer, he says, "The Grand Pacific at The Montclair is still available."

"No!"

If I show up there, Mrs. Ruiz will think I'm reporting for work. I can't imagine what lie I could concoct for why I would be accompanying Mr. Lee into his suite. But I don't want to go back to my place either. There's not enough privacy, and I don't know that he wants to slum it.

He pushes a button on the car's dashboard, and a woman's voice comes on over the speaker. She speaks in Chinese, and Tony answers in Chinese. She replies, then hangs up.

I stare out the car window. My heartrate matches the speed of the car. Is this really happening? Did I just finagle him into having sex with me? Either way, he doesn't seem happy about it.

What have I done?

CHAPTER TWELVE

The woman Tony called earlier on speaker calls back, and I hear the word "Drescott" amidst the Chinese.

Once in the city, he drives toward Union Square. The Drescott is a high-end boutique hotel just blocks from the shopping district comprising Neiman Marcus, Burberry and Tiffany's—stores I don't even go inside to gawk.

Pulling up in front of the Drescott, he hands the keys to the valet, who opens my door and gets my duffel bag. Taking my elbow, he guides me into the well-appointed lobby. This is not a place one rents by the hour, but that's what we're going to do. As he goes up to the check-in, I hang back because Tony and I do not look like we go together.

"Just one night, Mr. Lee?" the receptionist asks.

"Yes," Tony responds.

"Ricardo here can get your bags for you."

"That won't be necessary."

Card key in hand, Tony approaches me and we walk together to the elevator.

"I didn't mean for you to have to book a hotel room," I say with guilt as the elevator climbs to the top floor. Maybe I should be offering to pay for the room, or at least half of it? But I don't have the twenty thousand dollars yet.

"Where else is this supposed to happen?"

I guess we could have gone back to Eric's place, but by then, Tony might change his mind.

"My best friend from high school did it in the back of her boyfriend's pickup truck," I tell him.

"I don't want a mess in the back of the Porsche."

Oh. It's not the most romantic response, but it's practical.

We step out of the elevator, and he opens the door to a suite. It's not as fancy as the penthouse in The Montclair, but it's more luxury than I could ever afford.

He drops my duffel bag on the sofa and puts his sunglasses on an end table. Staring at me, he takes out his cigarette case.

Remembering the sign by the door, I say, "I don't think this is a smoking room."

I regret ruining his fun, but billionaires should follow the same rules as everyone else. He presses his lips together and puts away the cigarette case.

We stand several feet apart, staring at each other. Suddenly, I remember I never did work out the condom issue. "Um..."

How do I say this?

"About protection..." I manage.

He narrows his eyes. "You're not on birth

control?"

"I tried pills once, but they gave me terrible headaches. I didn't get around to exploring other options. And most of them don't protect against STDs anyway. I'm not suggesting that you have an STD, just that I don't know you that well—"

He picks up his sunglasses. "I'll be back in about twenty minutes. Relax. Order room service."

He leaves without telling me where he's going.

I sit down and contemplate what I should do next. Should I change into something more appropriate for the occasion? But what would that be? I don't have any sexy lingerie, and it's not like this is my wedding night.

I find the leather-bound room service menu. My eyes widen at the prices. I put the menu back.

Holy crap. This is happening. I'm going to have sex. For the first time in my life. With Tony Lee. Never in a million years would I have thought my first time would be with an international billionaire.

I don't move from the sofa the entire time he's gone. He returns with a bag from the local drugstore.

"Protection," he says, setting the bag down. "What did you order?"

"I didn't," I reply. "Everything was expensive."

He picks up the menu. "What do you like to eat?"

"I'm okay. I don't—"

"What do you like to eat?" he repeats.

"I'll try just about anything once."

He scans the menu. "You like scallops."

I nod. He picks up the phone and orders a mixed green salad, the scallops over linguini, a crème brûlée with Chantilly and blackberries, and a bottle of Château Latour.

After hanging up, he sits down on the sofa an arm's length away. He leans back and studies me. "What are you going to study at Berkeley?"

"I don't know yet. I was thinking of taking some sociology classes, maybe some education classes."

"Sociology? You can't make a lot of money in that field."

"Not everyone goes to college to get rich."

"College is an investment, supposedly. There's an expected ROI."

"ROI?"

"Return on Investment."

"But it doesn't have to be measured in dollars."

"How else would you measure it?"

"Well, there's value to society, to individuals. And personal fulfillment. You can't put dollar amounts on stuff like that."

"Actually, economists do."

"Is that why you went to college? To get rich?"

He curls a corner of his mouth. "I was rich before I went to college."

"To become even richer then?"

He shook his head. "I was just satisfying

expectations."

"Where did you go to college?"

"PSL. Paris Sciences et Lettres."

"What did you study?"

"Business and economics."

"Did you like it?"

He thinks for a moment. "It was okay."

"It must come in handy with what you do now."

"My brother wants that to be the case, but the family business is more his interest than mine."

"What kind of business is it?"

"Real estate and venture capitalism. My family were large landowners in Vietnam. We're also the main investors in a major tech company in Shenzhen looking to secure more defense contracts."

"Is that what you're meeting with Eric about?" I ask, hoping I don't sound nosy, but I like making conversation with Tony and getting to know the man I'm going to sleep with.

"He wants to pitch me on a real estate development."

"Do you like this kind of work?"

He doesn't respond right away. "It is as good as any."

"Is there something you would rather do?"

He gives me an odd look, as if no one has ever asked him that before. "I never really considered other options. There were times I didn't want to go into the family business and almost dropped out of college."

"My mother is a social worker. Maybe that's why I'm interested in the social sciences, though I wouldn't call social work a family business."

The mood between us has lightened. He asks about my family. I explain that my parents adopted me when I was a toddler. Lila was my caseworker, and every time she came to check on me, I'd cling to her leg and cry when she left.

He asks next about my birth mother, whom I know relatively little about, just that she was born in North Carolina, came out to California and got married, then became a dental hygienist. I had come out West to see if I could get to know her. Not that I felt the need for a mother. Lila filled that role better than anyone for me. But I did want to understand why my mother gave me up, and part of me had romanticized the possibility of becoming friends with her.

Room service comes a few minutes later. Not having eaten back at the house, I dig into the food, which is somehow even better than last night's dinner. Tony pours a glass of wine for me.

"How do you like it?" he asks after my first sip.

"It's good," I answer.

He studies the label. "At eight hundred dollars, it should be."

I nearly spit out my next sip. "God Almighty. You

shouldn't have."

"It's a somewhat special occasion, no?"

I blush. It's a kind gesture on his part, but I can't find the words to thank him.

"Aren't you going to have anything to eat?" I ask.

"I had lunch."

So the food was for me. The wine, too, and the hotel suite. I feel bad for having put him through this.

As if he knows what's on my mind, he says, "You can change your mind. It would be the smarter course of action."

I draw in a breath. "I said I'm okay with it. It's just, you didn't have to do all this—the hotel, the wine."

"You don't understand what I'm saying." He leans toward me, pinning me with his stare, his tone serious. "You *should* change your mind."

I blink, not sure what to say.

He continues. "I ruin things. And people. I'd ruin *you*."

CHAPTER THIRTEEN

It's not so much the words as the way he says them. I sensed that Tony had an edge almost from the moment I met him. Maybe it has to do with the BDSM he says he practices. Or maybe it's something else.

"It's not a big deal," I assure him. "It's not like in the olden days when losing one's virginity meant one was being deflowered and would be cast out of society."

He frowned. "That's not what I'm referring to, though deflowering young women is not my thing, either."

"So...what is your thing?"

His gaze searches mine before pulling back. He gets up from the sofa. "I need to make a call."

Wandering into the bedroom, he dials a number on his cellphone and begins talking in French. I dig into the scallops and watch him close the door.

I don't understand him at all. Half the time I wonder if I repulse him somehow. But I don't get the sense that's truly the case, even though I can't point to anything tangible as evidence.

He's on the phone for a while, so I decide to turn

on the television. I flip through the channels, briefly pausing on a cooking show, a home makeover, and the news, but nothing keeps my interest. I pick at the crème brûlée. An hour passes, and I wonder if Tony is taking a nap. I don't hear him on the phone anymore.

I get off the sofa and walk to the double doors that lead to the bedroom. I put my ear to the door but hear nothing. Gently, I turn the handle and crack open the door. I glimpse the bed, and it's empty. Opening the door farther, I see that the balcony doors are open. Tony sits outside overlooking the bustle of people below.

I walk up to the balcony doors. "I saved some of the food for you."

He spares me a brief sideways glance. "You can finish it. I'm not hungry."

"Mind if I join you?"

He doesn't say no, so I take the other chair on the balcony. We sit in silence. Why is this so hard? If doing it with a virgin is such a big deal that men would shell out big bucks for, why isn't Tony jumping at the chance? Is some kind of old-fashioned chivalry holding him back?

"Have you changed your mind?" he asks softly.

"No," I reply, staring at him. "I'm ready to do it now. But...it seems like you've changed *your* mind."

"I'm no good for you, and you're no good for me."

"I get that I'm not your first choice, but if you give

me a few pointers, I'll do my best to make it good for you."

With a groan, he gets up and walks back inside. I follow. He stands with his back to me.

"You're a nice girl, Virginia Mayhew Porter. You should just take the money and focus on going to Berkeley."

"I'm not a girl."

"Pardon. Woman."

"Is it really the age? Is that what bothers you?"

He lets out a breath and runs his hand through his hair. "Yes, that's part of it."

I step closer to him. "You're lying."

The next thing I know, I'm slammed up against the wall, and he's invading every inch of my space, his arms caging me in. If he leaned down any farther, our foreheads would touch. A vein near his temple throbs.

"Why do you want this so much?" he snarls.

My breath is still lodged in my chest, but I manage to respond, "I don't know...I just want it to be you."

His pupils lose some of their constriction, and his body relaxes. I think he's about to release me, and I start to breathe at the prospect of freedom. But I'm wrong.

His mouth crushes mine, hard and unrelenting. The surprising force of it would have given me whiplash if not for the wall behind my head. I feel like I'm drowning, only I don't want to come up for air. The kiss hurts, but my body has caught on fire. Only more, not less, will do.

His hand cups the back of my neck, drawing me closer into him as his mouth smothers me. He parts my lips, making my head spin when his tongue dips into my mouth.

When he finally parts from me, my lips continue to burn. They continue to ache.

His pupils dilate, making his eyes darker even though they shine with emotion. He seems to appraise my reaction. I'm nervous, but I know what I want. I want more of him.

I tilt my chin higher, trying to reach his mouth. He doesn't move, and I feel like I've failed some test. I try to move my body closer, a stronger hint, but he grabs both my wrists and pins them above me to the wall. His breaths are hard, mine are shallow. We're in some kind of heady limbo charged with passion.

A thrill shoots through me as I realize he just might want this as much as I do.

And then he kisses me. It's not the brutal kiss from seconds ago, but it's not entirely gentle either. It doesn't matter. The pressure of his mouth on mine is all that I want. His lips roam over mine, claiming, releasing, tasting, lingering. I can't keep up, but I exalt every nuance. I can't remember ever being kissed like this before. Part of me feels like I can do this forever, the other part isn't content with just kissing. My body wants to drink in his in every way possible.

Unconsciously, my body strains toward him. He responds by pressing me into the wall with his body. I welcome the discomfort from being sandwiched between two forms of hardness because it distracts me from the fire raging within me, that threatens to burn any last bit of prudence urging me to heed his earlier warning.

As if he's worried that he's been too rough, he lightens the kissing, taking soft mouthfuls of my lips. He's gentle, almost reverential. But I'm beyond that. My desire doesn't have the patience. I don't have any room to maneuver, but I try to grind my hips against him. He senses this and deepens the kiss. His tongue seeks mine. I tried to be an equal partner in this dance but probably come across a little awkward.

He drops one of my wrists to cup my jaw, holding me in place as he takes over the dance with sheer force. I let him do what he wants, though it's not like I really have a choice. Beneath my waist, I'm a molten mess.

Releasing my jaw, he drifts his hand down my collar and pushes my sweater off one shoulder. He grasps my bare shoulder, making every nerve come to life with his touch. His hand slides down my back and comes to rest on the small of my back, where he presses me into the hardness at his crotch.

I guess I'm out of practice because my mouth is a little tired from being worked over by him, but there's no way I want him to stop.

His hand moves to my butt. Cupping a buttock, he crushes me to his groin. I lose my breath.

My back arches because even as our hips are joined, he still has my other wrist pinned to the wall. He lets me catch my breath, moving off my lips, kissing and sucking his way down the side of my neck to the shoulder he bared. He finally releases my other wrist and picks me up by the back of my legs. I'm shoved against the wall again with my legs wrapped around his hips. I circle my arms around him and nibble on his earlobe. He thrusts at me, making me wetter and wetter.

I hold him tightly as he carries me to the bed and sits down with me on his lap. Wanting the taste and feel of his mouth again, I brush my lips against his. His hand shoots to the back of my head, holding me in place as he maneuvers me into the angles he wants, pressing his desire into my mouth.

By now my body is going crazy, craving a deeper connection, ardor to ardor. Unlocking his lips from mine, he peels off my sweater and studies the rise and fall of my chest. He brushes the knuckles of one hand below my collarbone before caressing my neck and massaging my nape.

I revel in his every touch, eager to know how he will touch me next. Will it be soft and tender or hard and demanding?

He slides his fingers underneath the spaghetti straps of my camisole and pulls them down my arms till the top bunches beneath my bra, which he unhooks before I'm able to stop him. The bra springs off, revealing my perky but small breasts. I hope he's not super disappointed.

He doesn't seem to be, and cups a breast. He fondles the flesh, rolling and kneading the orb. My nipple hardens beneath his palm. He grabs me by the waist, lifting me, as he trails his mouth from my collarbone, between my breasts, and down toward my navel as he leans me back into the bed. Next come my jeans, which he slowly unbuttons and unzips, pulls down past my hips and legs, and drops on the floor. He does the same to the camisole, leaving me naked but for my panties.

He kisses his way up my inner thigh, making me gasp when he nears my crotch. His fingers brush against my underwear as he lays beside me. I am tense with need, with desire throbbing between my legs.

His hand grazes my abdomen, then slips into my panties.

My breath catches as his fingers nestle between my folds. Slowly, gently, he rubs me. I am so wet down there, I don't know what to do with myself. So I lie still and quiet as he strokes my flesh. His forefinger and middle finger slide down either side of my clit. I shiver.

God Almighty.

He starts to ply my clit, creating satisfaction and longing at the same time, masturbating me better than I can myself. I glance briefly at him. He stares at me, taking in every flutter of my lashes, every shaky exhale. The intensity is too much. I close my eyes and immerse myself in the scintillation of his fondling.

He slides his fingers over my clit, and I gasp aloud. After exploring a bit, he finds a spot that has me groaning. His fingers dig in, petting, rubbing, teasing. Tension, hot and heavy, starts collapsing into that spot. Sensing the implosion imminent, I grasp the bed linen. My brow furrows, and my body hangs upon a precipice.

And with a cry, I burst into convulsions, my mound bumping into his hand, legs trembling, back arching.

My clit is super sensitive now, but there's a last bit of hunger that he attends before the fondling finally fades. I lay flooded in bliss, which bursts like little bubbles in my veins. I release a shaky breath and open my eyes to find Tony gazing down at me.

Now comes the hard part.

CHAPTER FOURTEEN

I'm excited but nervous when he pulls my panties down. I'm completely naked while he still has all his clothes on. Should I be trying to undress him? I don't remember being this indecisive the few times I messed around as a teenager. Is it because I'm about to lose my virginity? Or is it because of *him*? He's in charge, and I don't want to risk screwing it up.

Pushing apart my legs, he settles between them. His hands glide softly over my thighs. This is it. It's going to happen. Should I remind him that the condoms are in the other room?

But he doesn't undo his pants. Instead, he's still leaning on the bed, his head inches from my mound. He circles my clit with his thumb. My body responds with renewed warmth. And then his head lowers farther.

Oh. He's going to do *that*.

I'm uneasy. The one boyfriend I had who gave it a try lasted two or three minutes down there. He had suggested I give myself a trim. I only take care of that during the swim season, so I haven't groomed that area in some months now.

Tony licks me next to my clit, and my breath leaves me. He does it again, the side of his tongue grazing my clit. The sensation is different from the caress of his fingers, but it's just as pleasurable. He teases me with light, languid licks. I'm sure I don't know how to breathe anymore.

Will my pubic hairs bother him the way they bothered my ex-boyfriend? Is it too wet down there for him? What about the scent?

"Relax," he tells me, caressing an outer thigh with his hand.

I try to push the questions out of my head and do as he says. His tongue does feel amazing. And...oh...he found the spot. Desire simmers there, waiting and wanting to burst into flames again. He flicks his tongue at it, coaxing and enticing my arousal in almost methodical measure.

Gradually my need to come surpasses any lingering self-consciousness. But instead of continuing what he was doing and taking me over the edge, his tongue moves lower to the base of my clit. It feels good there too, but I'm a little frustrated because my climax wasn't far away. He presses his tongue lower.

Whoa. There's another bundle of nerves there. I'm not sure if it's part of my clit, and it tickles at first, feeling vaguely like I need to pee. But I like it. I clench my core from being overwhelmed by the stimulation. I want to come, but I'm not entirely sure my body can handle it.

While his tongue fondles me, he presses his

thumb to my clit's go-to spot, and I am undone. The rest of my body has disappeared. I exist only between my legs, only the part he touches. A minute later, spasms hit my body hard. I let out a low wail as my body convulses on the bed.

When I come out the other side of the orgasm, still awash in ecstasy, I manage to finally relax. My sex throbs and my legs tingle, but I am able to breathe normally. I take in a deep breath and let it out in a contented sigh.

Tony stands up and wipes the moisture from his face with the back of his hand. He undoes his pants and takes out his cock. My ability to think hasn't fully come online, and I vaguely wonder how often he goes commando. I marvel at how hard he is, then worry a little. That thing is going inside me?

He tugs on his cock, and I see a glisten of cum at the tip. I wonder if I should go down on him, but he doesn't seem to expect anything from me as he continues with his hand job. I want to touch him. I want to feel that pulsing hardness, that evidence of his desire.

His other hand cradles his scrotum, pulling and occasionally squeezing his balls. Even now, his gaze is fixed on me. I decide not to move, as if doing so will startle him out of his arousal. I'm sure if he wants me to do anything, he'll let me know.

But is he planning on jerking himself off? If that happens, how are we supposed to have sex?

A few minutes later, a flush starts to spread across his chest and neck. His head falls back, his pelvis rocks, and cum spurts from him cock. He catches most of it in his hand, but a small amount lands on the bed next to me. I'm glad that he was aroused and able to have his own orgasm, but I'm also disappointed. I sit up and watch as he grabs a tissue and cleans himself off.

"Thank you for the, um, orgasms," I say, tucking a strand of hair behind my ear.

He inclines his head to the side as he looks at me, amused.

"So...is that it?" I ask next.

"We had sex, didn't we?" he returns.

"Yeah, but I thought..." I look down and murmur, "I thought we were going to go all the way."

Standing before me, he cups my chin and lifts my gaze to his. "You don't want me to be your first."

I sigh in exasperation. "Then what'd you buy the condoms for?"

"I changed my mind."

"Do you not want to do it with me?"

He drops my chin and seems upset. "Why don't you go take a shower. Then I'll take you home."

"I don't want to go home!"

Little fires appear in his eyes. "I don't do vanilla sex. And if you were my sub, that kind of behavior would land you in a lot of trouble."

I want to point out that what just happened was

surely "vanilla" relative to BDSM, but I don't want to anger him more, and I'm too frustrated to come up with a good response, so I stomp, a little petulantly, off to the bathroom.

I close the door and stare at myself in the mirror. My cheeks are still flushed from the orgasms. I know I don't turn a lot of heads, but I'm decently attractive. Talia's co-worker at the coffee shop seems to like me, and an older businessman at The Montclair once tried to hit on me. Sure, my breasts could be bigger and my ass smaller, but a lot of women would want my body. So why is Tony so resistant to me?

Shaking my head, I turn on the shower. I guess I'm not his type. He really does prefer non-virgins, Asians, or blonds.

But he couldn't be completely immune to me or he wouldn't have gotten it up at all, right?

Strange how, just days ago, I was perfectly fine with the state of my virginity, and now I'm not. I'm okay with losing my virginity to him, and either he doesn't believe me and thinks he knows better, or he simply doesn't want to do it with me. Which is it?

As I rub the hotel bath gel over me and rinse away the wetness between my legs, I decide I'm going to find out once and for all. If it's the latter, he's got to own up to it. If the former, he can take his patronization and shove it.

I slip into one of the hotel's super-fluffy robes and

walk out of the bathroom to see that Tony's out on the balcony again, opening his cigarette case.

"I think San Francisco law prohibits smoking within a hundred and twenty feet of a public building," I say.

"Are you some kind of smoking police?" he returns, putting away his cigarette case.

I glance down for a moment. "Mo—my father—died from lung cancer. He smoked."

"I'm sorry."

"He quit when I was adopted, but it was too late."

"You worried I'm going to die?"

"I wouldn't want anyone's life to be cut short if it didn't have to be."

He crosses his arms in front of him. "You don't know me. What if I'm a complete *connard*—asshole? What if I deserve to die?"

I consider the question before replying, "I *don't* know you, so I'm giving you the benefit of the doubt. Do you smoke a lot?"

"I grew up between Paris and Vietnam and spend a lot of time in China. Smoking is pretty popular in all those places. It's been said over half the men in China smoke, though Beijing has started cracking down on smoking in the past few years."

"I'd say there's a good number of smokers in North Carolina, but not as high as half the male population. There are a lot fewer smokers here in California for sure. Or, at least, I don't come across as many. Lila never let me touch a cigarette. Not even one of those e-things."

"All for the best." He uncrosses his arms. "You ready to go?"

I take a deep breath. It's shaky, but I manage to spit out the words clearly.

"I'm not going."

CHAPTER FIFTEEN

No reaction from him. Why does that make me more nervous?

"You want to stay at the hotel?" he asks calmly.

"I'm not leaving until...until we have sex."

Land sakes. I really said that.

His eyes steel. "We had sex."

"You know what I mean."

A muscle ripples along his jaw. He's not happy. This has got to be the craziest thing I've ever done. What was I thinking? But I can't walk back now. That would be wimpy.

"I want to go all the way," I add.

He closes his eyes in a rare show of vulnerability. When he opens them, I feel like I'm in a heap of trouble.

He strides over to me. "Your mother ever teach you to be careful what you ask for?"

"Sure. Look, I didn't just fall off the turnip truck—"

"The what?"

"Turnip truck. It's a Southern metaphor. It means I'm not naive, so stop treating me like a child."

He nods as if to say 'okay.' The next moment, I'm crushed to him, and his lips are bruising mine. He devours my mouth like he's starving, and it hurts. But in a good way because I have my answer. He wants me.

There are no tender kisses this time, no soft caresses. Only hard groping and brutal kissing. He shoves his hand between my legs. The rubbing has me instantly wet. With his lips still locked to mine, he works me till my sex is gushing, and I might as well not have showered. He rips open the knot in the bathrobe as if angry with it. He grabs a breast. The stimulation to multiple parts of my body sends my arousal through the roof.

Instead of gently laying me down on the bed like he did before, he pushes me down this time. He starts to unbutton his shirt. "You want to get fucked? Get ready to be fucked."

I brace myself. I'm nervous. Maybe I shouldn't have forced his hand this way. I shouldn't have upset him. But I've dug my own grave, now I've got to lay in it.

Remembering that the condoms are in the other room, he leaves to go get them.

Now is your chance, a small voice tells me. *You can lock yourself in the bathroom.*

But I remain motionless on the bed. I'm relieved that he remembered the condoms. I don't think I could have stopped him if he chose to proceed without. And that's when I realize that my actions were risky.

He dumps the contents of the bag on the bed: a box of condoms and a tube of lubricant. After undoing his buckle and pants, he strips them off. He's now fully naked, and he looks great: chiseled, masculine, but not bursting with beef like some heavyweight bodybuilder. He's perfectly proportioned and his skin is completely unblemished and even except for what looks like a scar on his left pec. If I weren't so nervous, I might work up the courage to touch him, to run my fingers over the planes of his chest and the ridges of his sixpack.

And then there's *that*. The stiff pole between his legs.

His body hovers over mine. I want him to kiss me again, but his mouth aims for my breasts. He grasps one harshly, making me gasp, then gives me a few teasing licks on the nipple before covering the hardened nub with his mouth. The heated pressure on my sensitized nipple makes my sex throb. I need something to spear the ache between my legs.

He lays atop me but props himself up on his elbows. I savor his weight upon me. I can feel his erection between us. The skin to skin contact makes it even more real.

A cool wind blows in from the balcony, but his body heat coupled with my arousal keep me warm.

He claims my lips once more, but it's more controlled this time. His tongue delves deep into my mouth, entangling with mine. My head spins with pleasure. I don't remember enjoying the act of kissing with this much fervor, but maybe that's because it's been so long. Or maybe it's him and the way he kisses: domineering but not stifling, passionate but not messy. It melts and agitates my insides. I can't get enough, yet the tension building between my legs wants more than kissing.

He cups the side of my face and tilts my chin with his thumb. He knows exactly how he wants my mouth positioned beneath his. He gives me room to return his kiss, and I savor the heat of his mouth, the taste of his lips and tongue, glad that he hasn't smoked. My hips press up toward him, wanting to grind my ardor against him.

His mouth moves down beneath my jaw and latches onto my throat. My back arches, and my nipples graze his chest. While kissing and lightly sucking my neck, his hands caress and grope my breasts, my waist, my hip, my buttock. I cry out when he starts to suck hard on my nipple. It's a little too much pressure. No, it's bearable. I like his mouth on my body. Surprisingly, the discomfort stokes rather than diminishes my arousal. He increases the pressure of his sucking. I gasp, then sigh with relief when he stops sucking to tongue the sensitive nub instead. But then he's back to sucking.

My hands grasp his shoulders, but I don't push him away. He kisses my nipple, providing fleeting seconds of respite, before attacking the bud once more. My nipple has never felt so hard in my life. The alternation between the barely-bearable sucking and light licking drives me crazy.

His hand slips between my thighs as he addresses my other nipple. I dread and want his attention at the same time. His thumb works its magic on my clit, and either my other nipple has a higher pain threshold or the pleasure fanning from my clit distracts me from his intense sucking and licking. My body's a mess from his assault. My patience thins. I want him inside me.

But he takes his time stroking me. He kisses his way back up and brushes his lips against my ear.

"You better be sure you want this," he murmurs.

I do! I do! Especially when you touch me like that...

But I manage to sound halfway composed when I reply, "I'm sure. You don't have to keep checking as if you need a signed and notarized consent form."

I'm not exactly sure where that sass came from. Maybe it's nerves. Maybe it's my eagerness. He didn't expect it either and raises his brow. His hand grasps my jaw, a little too tight for comfort. "That kind of impertinence could land you a world of pain, *ma petite*."

I'm not positive what he just called me. Some kind of harmless term of endearment, I'm guessing.

His French accent makes it sound super sexy, whatever it is. But I'm more focused on the phrase "world of pain."

His cock presses against my thigh, tantalizingly close to the void I need him to fill. I could simply lay back and enjoy his fondling, allow the rapture from it to take me to carnal heaven, but my body yearns for a more significant joining of the bodies, of him and me becoming one.

My lashes flutter beneath his piercing gaze, and my impudence turns into a soft plea. "Please."

"Please?"

"Please do it."

He replaces his thumb with the tip of his cock and moves it gently along my clit. I inhale sharply. He's so very close now to being inside of me. And it feels so good. He strokes himself against me, sometimes dipping lower, teasing the folds below until I whimper and squirm.

"You want this badly, do you?"

"Yes."

I'm going to go crazy if he doesn't... Feeling the head of his cock at my opening, I brace myself.

"Breathe out," he tells me.

I do so as he parts me down there. He's probably not even halfway in but it feels like a semi is trying to park itself in a spot reserved for compact cars.

Holding himself in place, he fits his thumb between our bodies and finds my clit. Because I don't want him to stop, I mask the pain of having my most intimate spot split open.

Stoking the arousal until I'm ready to take more of him, he slides more of his cock into me, stretching me, filling me. He claims my lips tenderly. I am one hot mess of conflicting sensations. The pain has receded but it's still there. Lust burns as strong as ever. With his fondling, he coaxes my ardor to take the reins. My craving for relief overtakes any and all discomfort. Gradually, he begins to move inside me. He mutters what I think is an oath in French.

His movements renew the pain, but desire has grown stronger. I'm ready to burst down there. As if allowing me to breathe unhindered, he has stopped kissing me. My eyes are closed as I relish the sensation of being filled by him, but I can feel him staring down at me.

I've come across the occasional porn video. One of my exes had a bunch of them saved on his computer. Tony's motions aren't at all like the jackhammer sex I've seen in porn. Despite the few glimpses of roughness, Tony's movement are surprisingly tender. Once again, pleasure boils between my thighs. My body takes in more of him, wanting the discomfort to take the edge off my intense desire. I grind against him. With a groan, he sinks deeper. He flicks my clit more fervently. I am hurled, shaking and crying, into the arms of orgasm.

I'm amazed that my body can find such bliss after the initial pain. I know from talking to other women that not everyone climaxes their first time, and I feel pretty darn lucky. I couldn't know for certain what Tony would be like in bed. But I had wanted him so badly, it didn't matter. He didn't have to see to my orgasms, and I'm grateful he filled my first time with exquisite pleasure. In the end, he was the right guy to lose my virginity to.

When I settle down from my euphoria and open my eyes, however, I take back my thoughts of gratitude. There's a look in his eyes that makes my breath catch in my throat.

CHAPTER SIXTEEN

"You don't think we're done, do you?"

I'm still in a post-coital daze, so I don't ask him what he means by that.

I notice he still feels hard inside of me, and when he slowly withdraws, I see that his cock hasn't softened one bit. There's blood on the condom, my thighs, and the bathrobe beneath me. I blush, thinking about the maid that has to deal with the dirty linen.

He looks up from the blood and into my eyes.

"I'm okay," I answer his unvoiced question. I feel raw and sore between the legs, but it doesn't bother me.

"Good."

Without warning, he flips me onto my stomach. He pulls me up to my knees by the hips. I panic at first because my face is buried in the bed, then flush because my ass is facing him. Though I'm lean, I manage to have a rounded backside. I would much rather have that extra flesh in my boobs, even though Lila always told me God made me perfect the way I am. Even Andre, overhearing me ask a friend if my butt looked big in a certain pair of jeans, chimed in to say he was proud he had a sister who's "got back." But I don't find much comfort in the lyrics of Sir Mix-a-Lot or the opinions of a younger brother, no matter how much I love Andre.

And, oh God, Tony's studying my ass. I've managed to turn my head to see him on his knees behind me, his head slightly tilted as he stares at my butt. The other day I thought a pimple might be forming on my right butt cheek because my new underpants had shrunk in the wash and kept rubbing against me. I hope there's not a zit on my butt.

Tony caresses a buttock, and I decide maybe it's better I don't look. He grabs several pillows and puts them beneath my stomach to prop me up. Then he grabs my wrists and holds them behind my back with his hand. He taps his cock against my derrière, and for a second, I worry that he's going to take my back entrance. I never agreed to anal sex, and in my current position, with my hands pinned behind me, there's nothing I can do to stop him. But his cock slides into my wet slit.

O. M. G.

The stretching still hurts, but not as bad as the first time he penetrated me. And there's something about this angle, the areas within me that he touches that is positively *exquisite*. He brushes his free hand along the arch of my back. Then, still holding my wrists, he wraps his other hand around my hip to fondle my clit. I am in some other heaven. It's like my clit exists inside and outside of me. If it weren't for the orgasm waiting for me at the end, I'd want to stay in this place forever.

I groan in appreciation, in pleasure, in excitement. There's something more naughty, more titillating about this position. I shiver when Tony bucks lightly against me.

He seems to sense my wonder because he remarks, "Never thought you'd like doggy-style this much?"

He works my clit until I'm ready to explode. I thought I was perfectly satisfied after the last orgasm, but now I'm starved again.

But he withdraws his hand from between my legs and presses his cock deeper inside. My legs quiver. My clit pulses. Tension is coiled below my belly. He starts a steady thrusting, dragging his cock through me in a way that sends flutters of delight through my loins. I almost can't stand how good it feels. He touches me between the legs again, and within seconds, I am convulsing. I exhale a high and ragged cry as rapture somersaults inside my body. He thrusts harder, deeper, plowing ecstasy against my body until I am tempted to beg him to stop.

He straightens and slams his hips into my ass.

God Almighty.

I didn't realize how much he had been holding back till now. It's not about me or my body anymore. He's seeking his own release, using my body to hurl him to where I just returned from. My teeth chatter from the force of his thrusts. The sound of his grunting, of his pelvis smacking loudly into my backside fills my ears. He exchanges depth for speed. I'm not sure which is easier to take, but now I know what it means to be fucked hard.

He drives me into the bed, and after a few final thrusts, I hear him roar and feel him tremble. He bucks more gently against me before he finally releases my wrists. His cock pulses furiously inside of me. My body has never received a pounding like that before. At times it hurt as much as when that line drive in softball struck me in the leg. But I'm glad for him, glad he achieved his fulfillment and that I had played a part.

After withdrawing, he collapses onto the bed next to me and pulls me to him.

"*Pardon*. I'm sorry if I went too hard," he says after blowing out a breath.

"It's totally fine," I reply. It's not a hundred percent true, but, as Mowould often say, it's good enough for jazz.

Tony seems contemplative, and when he speaks, his words carry an ominous tone. "You're going to wish you heeded my warning."

*****

I like being curled beside him, and I don't want to talk about buyer's remorse. I assume that's what he's referring to. Anyway, I decide to ignore his words. My gaze sweeps over his body, gorgeously tan, gorgeously masculine. I run a hand over his pecs and down his six-pack. Unlike me, he could be a model. It's not just his looks and muscles that would make him a good one. It's his posture, his devastating gaze, and the way he carries himself. Eric Drumm is taller, but he comes across as a kid next to Tony.

"Why did you wait until now to lose your virginity?" Tony asks.

I shrug. "I wasn't waiting for the love of my life, if that's what you're wondering—or worried about. I'm not romantic like that."

"Really? I find most American women tend toward romantic."

"Well, I can't draw any comparisons as I grew up here in America and never traveled abroad, but Lila was practical, almost to a fault. I never went through a princess phase like most girls because Lila didn't want me to think that the end-all-be-all was sittin' in a castle waiting for Prince Charming to come along."

"And I'm hardly Prince Charming."

"Well...I don't think Prince Charming would smoke." I raised myself up to look into his eyes. "You ever thought about quitting?"

He narrowed his eyes. "You're not about to lecture me on the demerits of smoking."

"What if I did?"

"I won't hold back the next time I fuck you."

Good Lord. He had been holding back? I shudder, imagining what it would be like if he went all out. I don't think my body would hold together.

"Then I'll just assume you know already that smoking is bad for your health," I say. It was a little risky, but I was just returning a little of his own patronization. 'Course, he might not see it that way. And if he did, he might not care.

"I'm no good for you, but that hasn't stopped you."

"Do you really care what happens to me?"

His jaw tightens. "I shouldn't."

"Right," I say after a pause. "You don't know me. Maybe I deserve what I get."

"I could say that I'm giving you the benefit of the doubt, but I can tell you're no asshole. Assholes don't try to return umbrellas because they're worried some rich son of a bitch might get wet."

"And the fact that you would warn me against you shows that you aren't a complete asshole either."

"But that doesn't mean it's wise to have sex with me. What were you thinking?"

"What do you mean?"

"Look, I can tell you're a nice girl—"

I bristle.

"Woman," he corrects, "but what you did was stupid. Just because you wanted the money—"

"Lots of women trade their body for money."

He gives me a hard look. "And most of the time, they're forced into it. You may not have been raised a Cinderella, but you're as naive as one."

I think about the stories I've read about sex trafficking, of little girls in Thailand giving blow jobs to travelers from the West, of women smuggled into the United States to work in the sex trade. Like Tony said, they're forced into it. Or they live in such poverty, they have to turn to prostitution just so that they don't starve to death. But I'm not ready to accept his assessment that I'm stupid.

"I'm not this privileged person who has no idea that the world can be a bad place," I say. "I grew up in the South with *black* parents. I saw a lot of crap."

"And you still thought it would be okay to sell your virginity to a stranger?"

"You don't want me to lecture you about the dangers of smoking, but you want to lecture me about what I did?"

"I know that smoking is dangerous for my health. I know that it's turning my lungs black. Do you fully comprehend the danger you risked doing what you did? I didn't have to go get condoms. And if I decided not to, you couldn't have done anything about it."

I weigh the truth of what he says. I was taking a big risk. What if I had ended up with Eric Drumm instead of Tony? I'm pretty sure I wouldn't be as pleased.

"Okay," I concede. "I got lucky."

"Maybe."

"Maybe? I know it could have been ugly. I *fully comprehend* I could have gotten myself into real trouble."

Tony shook his head. "You are in trouble."

While I ponder what he means, he adds, "You have no idea what I want to do to you."

CHAPTER SEVENTEEN

Disgruntled, Tony pulls off the condom and gets out of bed. "I need to smoke."

"Wait," I say. "Isn't there something else you can do? Like, watch tv or have a glass of water?"

"If you smoked, you'd know that those are poor substitutes for a cigarette."

I hurry through various ideas and land on, "A blow job. Would that be better than smoking?"

He stares at me. "Are you offering?"

"Sure. Especially if it'd help save your life."

"You've given many blowjobs before?"

"Some."

"How many?"

"Four or five... maybe three. I haven't had any complaints."

Walking over, he lifts my chin and studies me. I stare back into his almond shaped eyes, wishing I knew how to read them. He lets go. "All right. I won't go for a smoke. We'll shower, then get you home."

Wait. He's still planning on taking me home? After all that happened? What about the things he wants to do me? I watch him walk into the bathroom and turn on the shower. I'm not ready to go home. I want to see if I can understand those dark eyes of his. I want to get to know him more, to find out why it is I can simultaneously feel safe and scared with him.

I hear him step into the shower. I don't get it. One minute he looks like he wants to devour me, the next he wants to get rid of me. Something tells me I should take advantage of the latter sentiment, but I'm the proverbial moth drawn to a flame. Which means I'm not acting practical despite my claim. I'm not harboring any romantic notions about Tony. He and I are from such different worlds, but maybe that's what makes him interesting to me. I want to explore him more. Temporarily. I don't expect to relocate into his world. I just want to be a visiting tourist.

I roll my eyes at my own metaphor and head into the bathroom. He's already beneath the shower, water raining over his head and body. As the glass isn't frosted and only partially encloses the shower, I can see everything. His butt is absolutely delicious. I've never been a butt person. Till now. The muscles are taut but the flesh is supple enough to sink one's teeth into.

When he turns around to see me, he pauses, then steps aside, a wordless invitation. I step into the shower, feeling giddy, as if we hadn't just had sex together for the first time. He lathers up his hands and applies the soap to my shoulders, gently washing me. My heart skips several beats when his hands move across my breasts, down my belly, and to my pelvis. His fingers comb my pubic hairs before spreading my thighs. He wipes away the blood there before finishing my legs. Turning me around, he washes my back and ass, and a familiar warmth stirs within me. God, how is he able to turn me on so much?

Taking the removable shower head in hand, he rinses my body. I gasp when the water streams between my legs, hitting the folds between them.

"You ever use one of these on yourself?" he asks.

I nod, a little embarrassed at admitting a fact I haven't even shared with my roommates, though I'm pretty sure they've used the shower head for secondary purposes as well.

He adjusts the angle of the showerhead so that the water hits my clit. I close my eyes and bask in the pleasant sensations. While holding the showerhead in one hand, he massages my right breast with his free hand. I groan and begin to think he can do anything to me and my body will respond. I even relish the soreness in my vagina. It's sore because of him. As Talia would say, I can move on to better things now that I've gotten my virginity out of the way.

Slowly but surely, the pelting of the water against my flesh builds me toward my climax. He kneads my breast, tugging on the nipple, for a few minutes more before dropping his hand to my mound. His fingers part the labia, allowing the water to hit me more fully. I groan more as he moves the showerhead even closer to me. With a soft cry, I erupt.

I make a mental note to get the brand name of this particular showerhead. It's a lot more effective than the one in my apartment. Or maybe it has nothing to do with the showerhead and everything to do with who's holding it.

"Okay, okay," I squeak when I can't take any more of the stimulation of the water against my overly sensitized parts.

He holds the showerhead in place a few more seconds before returning it to its mount. He stares at me as I let out a long sigh and gaze up at him through glazed eyes. Still pulsing madly between my thighs, I notice his cock is half erect.

"Your turn," I say, grabbing the soap.

He lets me wash him, and my hands happily traverse every inch of him, except for his cock, which is now fully erect. I drop to my knees and marvel at how flesh so soft can harden into something as if it's a limb with bones. Gingerly, I wrap my hand around him. His cock pulses upward with my touch.

Sticking out my tongue, I like his tip. He grunts when my tongue slides under his crown. Hungry for him, I take more of him into my mouth. I relish his moan. Feeling empowered, I begin to suck. Steam curls around us, and little rivers of water run down his body. I take another inch and feel his hand at the back of my head. I draw my mouth up his length, then back down. I do this several more times and hear the rumble of appreciation in his throat.

I try to take him in deeper, which he encourages by pressing the back of my head. I try not to gag when he pushes me too far, but it's hard not to. It's been a while since I've given a blow job. He lets me come off him to gather myself, but I don't want to come across totally incompetent and get back on his cock quickly.

"Suck it harder," he commands.

I do as he bids till he's murmuring in a foreign language again. He pushes me deeper down his cock. I start to choke when his tip hits the back of my throat, but this time he doesn't let me come all the way off. My mouth gets to the flare of his crown before I am pushed back down. His black pubic hairs tickle my nose. I go back up his shaft for some relief and brace my hands against his hips. But he's stronger and shoves me back down. This time the water running down his body splashes over my face. For a second, I can't breathe until he lets me back up his cock. My reprieve is short-lived. Once again he shoves me into his crotch. Water pours over me.

When I sputter and choke, he lets me come off. I

wipe my eyes and gather myself as quickly as possible. Without a second to waste, his cock is back inside me. I find my timing, taking my breath when I go up his shaft and holding my breath when I am smooshed into the water cascading over his groin. He hits my gag reflex several times, but he's past the point of slowing down. Gripping my hair, he pulls and pushes my head up and down his cock.

His hips get into the action so that it's a full-on fucking of my mouth and throat. I lose my timing and wonder if it's possible to drown while giving a blowjob. With a loud grunt, he bucks faster, and I taste salty heat on my tongue. Unprepared, I choke in earnest. He releases me, and a spurt of cum lands on my cheek as he pulls his cock out. He wraps a hand around himself and pumps the rest of his cum.

He bends down and lifts up my chin, gazing into my face as if to check that I'm okay. I give him a small grin.

"I hope that was better than a smoke," I tease.

"That was much better than a smoke," he acknowledges.

And the glimmer in his eyes tells me I have a chance at not getting sent home.

CHAPTER EIGHTEEN

As Tony and I step out of the shower and dress, I brace myself for the forthcoming argument. I decide to blow-dry my hair to give myself more time to think. He has no reason to keep me except for sex, and though I have a feeling that mine wasn't the best blowjob he's ever had, it was good enough. And he wants me. How much, I can't say for sure. But I glimpse the desire he tries to hide beneath half-lidded gazes. And I think a part of me had sensed it before or I wouldn't have been so bold with him. Knowing that he wants me even a little is as thrilling as everything else. I want this to last as long as it can because I know in a few days' time, he'll be gone. Back to China or Paris or Vietnam. And I'll probably never see him again unless I keep working at The Montclair. Even then, I can see us crossing paths with only the faintest acknowledgment of each other because he'll have some supermodel on his arm the next time.

But for the time being, I want to make him mine.

When I step out into the living room, I see him looking over my leftovers, now cold and not quite as appetizing. His hair is still damp, making him look even sexier.

"You want to go get something to eat?" I ask. "There's a great pho place near Chinatown. If you like pho. I don't mean to assume you do just because you're from Vietnam."

And maybe pho isn't fancy enough for billionaires.

"Pho sounds good," he replies.

I'm ecstatic as this means my getting taken home has been delayed. I suggest we walk because trying to find parking will be a pain in the butt.

"My driver's in the city," he offers.

"I don't mind walking," I say. "But if you prefer to drive or be driven..."

He grabs his jacket. "We'll walk."

"Do you usually get driven places?" I ask.

"No. My brother does just because he can get more work done that way, but I'm not that involved in the business. I don't have to make every minute count."

I nod but can't resist a little teasing. "So you can actually do things for yourself."

He raises his brows. I'm not sure if he's amused. I think he is.

"I'm not lazy because I can afford to have things like driving and meals done for me," he says, opening the door for me. "It's a matter of efficiency."

"I know. Like with your brother, the opportunity cost of him taking half an hour to make dinner would probably be in the thousands, or hundreds of thousands."

"Exactly."

"On the other hand, not every minute has to count. I mean to say, one doesn't have to think of every minute as lost revenue. There's value in not working as much as possible."

"You sound European."

"Well, I remember, when I was waitressing at Dee's, which is one of the best barbecue joints in the Tri-Cities, I had to serve this group of New Yorkers who were in town for business. They couldn't complain enough about how slow everything in North Carolina moved compared to New York. Maybe they just didn't understand that you don't rush good barbecue. And if you're going to have lunch at Dee's, you ought to enjoy your time there. Spending it complaining doesn't seem like an efficient use of the time God grants you."

"You might fit in in France. Dinner there can take three hours."

"Okay, things may move slower in the South but not that slow." I think for a moment. "But a super long dinner actually sounds nice. I would try that, a three-hour dinner. I'm usually scarfing down a sandwich in between work and classes, and I don't even taste or remember what I ate."

"You'd like it. You can savor your meal, and I see how much you enjoy food."

I blush. "I never thought I'd like scallops this much. Was it that obvious?"

"Your face lit up like a beacon."

I blush deeper. Maybe I should stay away from food in front of Tony.

"You light up during sex, too."

A woman walking into the elevator as we walk out turns her head. My face is probably as red as a cherry right now.

"Your emotions are easy to see," Tony says as we exit the hotel.

Unlike Mr. Pokerface next to me.

Tony turns enough heads just by being him, so I change the subject because I don't want more attention drawn our way. "The pho place is nothing fancy. In fact, it's a hole in the wall, but they serve great pho."

"You're a pho connoisseur?"

"Actually, I've never had pho till I came to San Francisco, and I wasn't a huge fan when I first tried it. But it's definitely grown on me. It's kind of like Asian comfort food: it's filling and affordable. It probably won't be as good as what you can get back in Vietnam. I'm sure it isn't. But I hope you like it. At least the options are much better here in San Francisco then back in North Carolina. I mean, we have ethnic food in Durham, in Charlotte, but it's a whole new level here in San Francisco. There could be more soul food options, though."

"Soul food?"

"Fried chicken, collard greens, sweet potato pie."

"Fried chicken is popular in China. KFC outperforms McDonald's quite a bit."

"I guess KFC is better than nothing, but that's not what I would call soul food. If you're interested, there's a pretty good place here in the city called Maybelle's. Her sweet potato pie's to die for."

Of course, we won't get to try it if he decides to end our time together, I want to point out but decide not to press the issue just yet.

We reach the pho place on the outskirts of Chinatown. It's before the dinner rush, so we easily grab a table in the corner. I pick up the plastic menu propped against a bucket of chopsticks and Asian soup spoons and jars of hot sauce, but I know I'm getting my usual, the Tái Gầu. Tony orders the noodle soup with fish balls, something I've never worked up the guts to try.

"How come you decided not to use your driver to Eric's place?" I ask after we order.

"I like to drive. When I was younger, I wanted to be a racecar driver."

"Did you change your mind or is it still something you want to do?"

"It wasn't an acceptable career path. Good Chinese boys go to good colleges," he replies tersely.

Somehow I don't see him as a "good boy." In fact,

his vibes suggest the opposite.

"That must've been hard giving up something you enjoyed doing."

"I didn't give it up completely. I raced without my father knowing. I stopped racing when my cousin died. We were racing Taike Road between Taiyuan and Jiaogu when her car spun out. I should have known she couldn't handle going into the "Devil U Shape" at my speed. But I was selfish. I wanted to take the turn fast even though I knew there was a chance she wouldn't slow down."

"I'm so sorry," I say quietly.

He blinks away the pain in his eyes and fixes the intensity of his stare upon me. "Did you say your parents were black?"

I nod. "Lila and Mo adopted me when I was three and a half. I don't remember much of my early years, but I remember hanging on to Lila's leg a lot. Mo said I didn't give her much of a choice but to adopt me."

"Was that unusual?"

"You know, it wasn't to black folk. At Lila's church, which was mostly black, I never felt out of place. It was more white folk who thought it strange. Actually, they usually assumed Lila was my nanny. But I remember when I was eight years old, and we were driving home from a restaurant, Mo got pulled over by a cop. He said Mo didn't come to a complete stop at the stop sign, but I was sure he *had*. He and

Uncle Ray often talked about how they have to drive extra careful because they could get pulled over anytime for a DWB."

"What is a DWB?"

"Driving While Black. The cop kept asking me if my parents knew where I was. I was so confused and scared. He told me he was going to call my parents for me. He didn't believe me when I said Lila and Mo were my parents. We had to go down to the police station, and I was placed with Child Protective Services. I thought they were going to take me permanently away from Lila and Mo. It was the scariest moment of my life, next to finding out that Mo had lung cancer and the time Andre got a concussion."

"Andre's your brother?"

"My parents adopted him when he was ten. He bounced around the foster system a lot. I want to go into social work because Lila made such a huge difference in my life and Andre's life."

"And she approves of your career preferences?"

"I think Lila would support me in just about anything—within reason. She probably wouldn't be too happy if I went into something like modeling—not that I would ever qualify to be a model—but even then she probably wouldn't strictly forbid it."

Prostitution on the other hand...

"Would she forbid selling your virginity?"

If Tony were polite, he wouldn't have addressed

the elephant I let in the room, but it didn't surprise me that he went there. Like I said, he didn't strike me as a "good boy."

"Well, there's nothing she can do about it now," I retort. "She would be mortified, and, yes, there was no way she would have let me do it. She'd work extra hours, all while suffering from arthritis and GERD, so that me and Andre could have the life we want. And I just—I don't want her to have to do that."

The bowls of steaming hot noodles arrive then, and I'm glad for the distraction. I'm not sure why I'm so chatty. Maybe sex makes me loquacious.

"I'm not sure how the French eat," I say as I prepare to dig in, "but I'm totally fine with slurping. My friend James Fan, who introduced me to pho says it's a must because you want to eat the noodles and soup when it's nice and hot, but you have to draw in air so you don't burn yourself."

"This James tell you anything else about pho?"

"Just that the sauces are a must, too."

We focus on eating, and after a few mouthfuls, I realize I'm not that hungry, having eaten earlier in the hotel.

"So how's the pho?" I ask.

"Good," he acknowledges as he adds more hot sauce into his bowl.

"Do you eat mostly French, Chinese or Vietnamese cuisine?"

"Depends where I am."

"Do you prefer one over the other?"

"Good food is good food."

"That's what Lila would say. My roommates and I went to this food truck festival last year, and it was amazing the different kinds of food there were. I tried a bite of Talia's Burmese fermented tea leaf salad. I wasn't crazy about it, but it was cool because I had never had Burmese food before."

"You're an adventurous eater."

"I don't know if I'm adventurous. Mostly curious. I'd love to visit the places the foods come from some day."

"How are you going to do that on a social worker's income?"

"I'm not sure. I could slum it, stay in hostels—"

Tony wrinkles his nose.

"I think it could be great. After all, it's the sights, the people, the food that I would be interested in. One doesn't travel around the world to stay in luxurious places."

"You say that because you haven't stayed in a truly luxurious place. Trust me, you're better able to enjoy the sights when you have a nice room waiting for you at the end of the day."

"I work in a luxury hotel," I remind him.

He leans closer. "The Montclair is nothing compared to the resorts we have in Vietnam, Thailand, and Bali."

"I can't imagine a place nicer than The Montclair." I shake my head and swirl my spoon in the soup. "But maybe that's a good thing. I can appreciate the less than finer things in life."

I give him a small smile, which he returns.

"So you're saying I'm spoiled," he says.

I think for a moment. "Possibly. That's the potential disadvantage of having experienced the best and most expensive things in life: everything else can seem disappointing by comparison."

"I'll take that disadvantage."

The lunch is over sooner than I'd like. The waitress leaves the bill, and I reach for my purse.

"Put it away," he commands.

"I can get this. It's the least I can do since you're paying for the hotel room and room service unless..."

"Are you serious? You were desperate enough for money that you were willing to sell your virginity—"

"For which I'm getting twenty thousand dollars," I say cheerfully. "Plenty to cover the pho."

"You don't have the money yet."

I decide not to argue with him. It's true I don't need to run up more debt on my credit card, even if it's only twenty bucks.

After leaving the restaurant, we head back to the hotel. I spend half the walk asking about his family, his travels, what he thinks of San Francisco, and the other half wondering how I'm going to convince him to let me stay with him.

CHAPTER NINETEEN

"I don't suppose we could stay the night?" I ask when Tony hands the ticket to the valet at the hotel to get his car. "Seems a waste to pay for a room and not actually use it."

"We used it, or don't you remember?" he returns.

"You really want to take me back?"

He looks at me as we wait outside the hotel. "I'm taking you home."

"So the, um—it wasn't good enough?" I venture to ask, then kick myself because the question makes me sound needy. "I know I'm not very experienced, but I'm a quick learner. And adventurous."

He emits a low groan. "I have made a decision."

"Don't you want the full value of your purchase?" I play with one of the buttons on my sweater. "Aren't there things you want to...do to me?"

He glares at me. "Yes, but they're not going to happen."

"Why not?"

"You don't understand."

"What do I have to understand? Tell me."

His eyes darken in a way that makes my breath stall. I want to look away but he's searching my eyes.

I don't know what he's looking for, but I want to convey more confidence than I feel, so I keep his gaze.

The valet returns with the car, and I don't get my question answered.

"Where do you live?" Tony asks after we get in the car.

I give him my address out in the western side of the city, which he punches into the car's built-in GPS. We pull away from the hotel, and I begin to resign myself that my time with Tony is coming to an end.

As we drive down Highway 280, I realize City College wouldn't be too bad of a detour.

"Could we make a quick stop to get my textbook?" I ask. "I left it in one of my classes. The college is right off Ocean Avenue"

I point southwest, and he exits the freeway. Once we get to campus, I have him pull up to Batmale Hall at a red curb.

"I'll be quick," I say as I open the door. "There's a parking lot—"

"If I get a ticket, I get a ticket," Tony says.

I nod. Must be nice not having to worry about things like parking tickets. Just before I make it into my classroom, I bump into Tracy.

She narrows her eyes at me. "I thought you were out sick?"

"I'm feeling better today," I respond. It's a true

statement.

"Mrs. Ruiz wasn't too happy that you missed work yesterday."

I can't tell if Tracy is saying that just to antagonize me or of it's true.

"I'll be back at work," I say even though it's really none of Tracy's business, but I just want to get my textbook and get back to Tony.

Stepping past her, I enter my classroom.

"Didn't see you in class this morning," Mr. Parker says as I gratefully accept my textbook from him. He tells his students we can call him Jeff, but I still think of him as Mr. Parker. Guess I'm old fashioned that way.

"I, um, had a work commitment that was hard to get out of," I reply.

"I uploaded the class notes. You can catch up that way, and I'll be doing extra office hours tomorrow."

"Thanks, Mr. Parker."

I hurry out the classroom and consider that the upside of Tony not wanting to finish out the week with me is that I get to focus on studying, which is what I'm supposed to be doing all along.

Even though Tony said he wasn't worried about a parking ticket, I worry for him, remembering how upset Mo once got at having to shell out an extra twenty-five dollars when all he needed was another quarter to prevent his meter from running out. And tickets in the San Francisco Bay Area are higher than twenty-five dollars. But a few yards from where Tony is parked, I run into James.

"Hey, Virginia," James calls. "You want to study for the econ test this weekend?"

I perk up at this offer. James sets the curve in class.

"Sure! But I don't think I'd bring much to the table since you know the material better than anyone else."

"Actually, you'd be helping me out a lot. It helps solidify things in my brain when I get to explain it to someone else."

I want to clap my hands and jump up and down. "I'd love to then."

"How about Saturday morning? At i-heart-boba?"

Boba is another Asian food item that James got me to try. It's amazing how many Asian tea places there are in the city. At the pace they're proliferating, they'll be reaching Starbucks density.

"I might be able to make that work."

"I'll text you."

"Thanks!"

I can't resist giving him a hug before heading over to Tony, who's leaning against the car waiting for me. Damn, but he seems to get hotter by the minute. I try not to dwell on that. At least I'll have some pretty good memories. I imagine how Talia will respond when I tell her I did it, I lost my virginity.

"Who was that?" he asks with a slight edge in his tone.

I open the door and climb into the car. "Oh, that's James."

"Your pho guy?"

"Yeah. We take econ together."

"You do anything else together besides econ and pho?" Tony asks as he buckles.

I look at him in bemusement. Could he possibly be jealous?

"No," I answer. "I mean, I guess we do boba together, but he's just a friend."

For some reason, Tony doesn't look like he believes me. I've never thought of James in a romantic way, but that's probably because I know he's gay. If he weren't...well, maybe. I could tell Tony that James is gay, but mischief prevents me. I kind of like the feeling that Tony might be a little jealous over little ole me.

"Your GPS isn't back on," I tell him even though I don't want to be taken home. I have about ten minutes to either change his mind or wrap up our arrangement.

"Don't need it," he replies.

"Thank you for the lunch—and the pho," I start. I can't remember having to have a more awkward conversation. I take a breath. "And for the...sex."

He doesn't say anything.

Not liking the silence, I continue, "I feel like I

kind of badgered you into it, but I had a good time and...I hope it wasn't all bad for you."

Still nothing. I want to tell him that I'm glad my first time was with him, but I don't want to come across too attached. I bet he has enough women smothering him, and I don't know if he's the type of guy who suffocates easily from a woman's attention, the kind of guy that freaks out if he senses a woman wants something 'more.'

It's weird, but it almost feels like *I* should be paying *him*. I was the one who wanted to lose my virginity. He wasn't chomping at the bit to take it.

"About the money...I just want to be clear that you don't have to pay it."

God Almighty, I'm crazy. I did this whole thing for the money. And it's not like twenty thousand dollars is going to break his bank. Far from it. But it's still not right. His wealth shouldn't devalue twenty thousand. It's still a lot of money, and he could do better things with that amount than give it to some scrawny chick he banged.

He glances over at me as if I'm two bricks short of a load, which I'm sure I am.

I hug my textbook to my chest. "It's just—it's an awful lot of money, and you've been really nice about it all."

He turns his gaze back to the road.

"I just don't feel like I did much to earn that kind of money," I say and decide I've probably said enough on the matter.

After several quiet beats, he finally says something. "Your virginity is not worth twenty thousand US dollars?"

"It's kind of silly to put a price on something like virginity. I guess if there's a market for it, then there's a role for price. Still, not everything can be boiled down to dollars and cents. Maybe I'll have a different perspective if I end up majoring in economics."

"So what would make you feel you had comfortably earned twenty thousand dollars?"

"I'm not sure. It's faster if you stay on Ocean Avenue," I tell him.

But he doesn't.

"Not for where we're going," he says with his gaze still straight ahead.

"Where are we going?"

"The Lair."

"What's that?"

"A place you can earn your twenty thousand."

CHAPTER TWENTY

I try to tamp down my excitement at the possibility he's changed his mind about taking me home. As he heads north, he speaks in Chinese to his phone. It dials a number.

A woman picks up the phone the call. "So nice to have your call, Mr. Lee,"

She knows his name? He must be a frequent or important visitor of this place.

"Is Cell Three available?" Tony asks.

"When do you need it?"

"In twenty minutes."

"It's all yours. For the rest of the day, if you'd like. We'll see you shortly."

Tony hangs up.

"What's The Lair?" I ask. I'm pretty sure it's not a restaurant or another hotel. What kind of place would have something called a 'Cell Three?'

"You're familiar with the Red Room from that book you're reading. The Lair is the Red Room times ten."

Maybe I shouldn't have asked.

"You go there a lot?"

"Only when I'm in town."

So his name pops up on their caller ID. It doesn't mean anything. I'm not even sure what goes on at this place. Some manner of BDSM.

Holy shit. It's one thing to read about it in a novel, another thing to be facing it for real. I look over and study Tony. I recall the different things he's said.

Fifty Shades...child's play.

You have no idea what I want to do to you.

I'd ruin you.

I'm nervous now. How much is he into BDSM? Does he know what he's doing? Is this something I'm willing to do?

The car pulls up before a three-story building. A woman in tight leather pants and 5 inch heels greets us. She opens my door and I step out tentatively, still clutching my textbook. I scan the building, as if I can find telltale signs of what happens inside. Tony hands her the car keys and, taking me by the elbow, guides me through the doors. We walk into a reception area with wainscoting, nicely appointed furnishings and potted plants. There's a set of stairs and curtains, but nothing indicates any nefarious activities.

Another beautiful woman greets us from behind a counter. "Mr. Lee, Cell Three is ready and waiting for you. Are you sure you don't want a room in The Upper Balcony instead?"

"That's where my cousin likes to play. I prefer the

dungeon."

Did he just say 'dungeon?'

She flashes him a smile. "Me, too. I just need you to sign your guest in. Would she like a mask?"

Tony answers for me. "Yes."

The woman brings out a tray of masks.

"What are these for?" I ask.

"You don't have to have one, dear," the woman says. "We pride ourselves on our discretion. Nonetheless, some people feel more comfortable with an added layer of protection for their identity."

I look over the selection and choose a simple mask of red silk and black lace. I realize I've brought my textbook with me, so the woman offers to help me put my mask on.

"We also request, for privacy reasons, that you leave all cameras and cellphones with me," the woman says.

I give her my purse, and Tony gives her his cellphone. Taking me by the elbow again, he leads me toward a set of stairs. I realize the building sits on a hill between two streets, so the downstairs is actually the floor level on the backside of the building. I wonder that Tony hasn't selected a mask for himself, but maybe it's not a big deal for him since he doesn't live in the country.

He stops at the top of the stairs and turns to me. "I can take you home and still pay you. The money is not an issue for me. The truth is I don't care if you take it or not. If you are foolish enough to refuse it, it's not my concern."

"But I'd feel better if I did more to earn it," I say. At least I hope that's the case.

"You may change your mind about that," he replies.

"I'll let you know if I do."

With that, he takes the stairs down. We enter a stark room with walls that appear to be the original concrete of the building. I gasp and nearly drop my textbook. In the middle of the room a completely naked woman lies shackled to the ground with her arms and legs each stretched to four different corners. Her mascara and eye liner are smeared because she's been crying. Dark pink lines mark her body. Above her stands a man wearing dark gloves and a hood. He holds a thin wooden cane, which he brings down across her thighs. She shrieks.

"Thank you, Sir," she murmurs between sniffles.

Changing the angle of the cane, he smacks it on the same thigh. The streaks of pink on her leg form an 'X.' He does the same to her other thigh, each strike eliciting a cry of pain from the woman.

"Thank you, Sir," she says again.

He squats down beside her head and rubs away a large tear that clings to the corner of an eye. She looks at him, her eyes shining with gratitude.

And reverence.

I look at the welts on her legs. Those aren't going

away in a few hours.

"You're doing good, slut," the man tells her. "You've earned a reward."

He stands up, puts the cane on a nearby table and returns with a cordless massage wand. The woman moans when he places it between her legs. Her eyes roll toward the back of her head.

"May I come, Sir?" she asks after a few minutes.

"Come, slut."

Her body starts to shudder, her limbs yanking at the shackles. The man pulls the wand away, and she sighs, a large grin plastered across her face.

"Thank you, Sir."

Because I was mesmerized with the scene, I don't know how long Tony has been staring at me. I can't make out his expression.

"Are they okay that we—that we were watching?" I whisper to him.

"Too late not to be," he replies.

I blush. I've never ever witnessed anything like this. Once, I accidentally walked in on Alexia making out with her boyfriend on the sofa in the living room. They were too involved to notice me, but I had quickly turned around and headed back to my bedroom anyway.

But here, I wasn't sure where to go except back up the stairs.

"Want to go home now?" Tony asks.

I pause and notice my pulse has quickened

considerably. I meet his gaze.

"No."

Taking me by the elbow again, he walks me past "Sir" and the woman on the ground. Tony pushes aside a black velvet curtain and we enter what I presume is "Cell Three."

There are no windows in this room, no paneling or paint to cover the concrete walls. A single overhead lamp lights the center of the room and leaves the rest in darkness. I start to doubt my marbles when I see a cage in one corner of the room, a human sized cross, a wooden pillory, and a case on the far side displaying a variety of canes like the one used by "Sir," floggers, paddles, and other striking implements. Beside the case is a tall lingerie chest. I'm not sure I want to know what's inside it. At least this room has a mattress, which has got to be more comfortable than being shackled to the cold hard floor. I hug my textbook tighter.

Tony studies my reaction to everything in the room. "I can take you home anytime."

I stare at a ring dangling from the ceiling. Curiosity wins the moment and I respond, "I don't want to go home."

Yet.

Tony takes off his jacket and hangs it on a hook on the wall. "I have simple rules: you ask permission when you want something, and you obey. Displease me, and I punish you. Simple."

Sure. Simple.

God Almighty.

He walks over to a table with a pitcher of water with slices of lemon and strawberry in it. He pours two glasses. "What are your soft limits? And your hard limits?"

I take the glass of water he hands me. I have no idea what my limits are. I just had sex for the first time.

"I guess we'll find out," he murmurs. "What would you like your safety word to be?"

Not knowing what would make a good safety word, I say the first thing that pops into my head. "Tar Heel."

He raises a brow.

"It's North Carolina's nickname: the Tar Heel State. Also the name of the athletic teams for UNC."

"What is a Tar Heel?"

"There are different legends. One says that troops from North Carolina during the Civil War stuck to their ranks like they had tar on their heels."

"Might turn out to be an appropriate safety word. Drink the water."

I take a few sips and turn to set it aside.

"Finish it," he orders.

"I'm not that thirsty—"

He frowns. "What did I say my rules are?"

I comb my memory. I'm usually not this forgetful, but my nerves are on overdrive.

"Ask permission," I remember. "And obey."

He waits as I finish my water. When I'm done, he takes the glass and my textbook. Without the latter, I don't know what to do with my hands, so I stuff them into my jean pockets.

Turning to face me, Tony leans against the table and crosses his arms. "Strip. Slowly."

My mouth turns dry. I liked it better when he undressed me. Standing here on my own, I feel like I'm on display.

"Now, Virginia."

I like the sound of my name with his accent. I remind myself that I wanted this.

Complying, I start to unbutton my sweater. I'm sure his gaze misses nothing. I peel off the sweater and hesitate at my plain V-neck tee. Okay, I was completely naked before him just a few hours before. I shouldn't be this uneasy.

But we're in a strange place, and there's a curtain instead of a real door guarding our privacy. Anyone can walk in on us at any minute. And it's one thing to be undressed by him while I'm half distracted by his caresses. Standing in the middle of the room while he watches has a totally different feel to it. I'm the center of attention. There's no other distraction. And I'm way too cognizant of his stare.

"The shirt," he prompts.

After taking a fortifying breath, I whip it off. Okay, this isn't too bad. And as much as his stare unnerves me, it also excites me.

"Jeans next," he directs.

I slip off my shoes, undo the button of my jeans and slowly pull down the zipper. At least I have on my nicest underwear and bra. They're burgundy colored with a little bit of ivory lace. I slide the jeans down my legs. I take off my socks just because it gives me something to do, something other than notice how his gaze traverses every inch of me.

"Turn around," he tells me, circling his finger.

Standing in just my bra and underwear, I feel the cool air on my skin while my body burns beneath his stare. My cheeks grow hot as I do a 360.

"Slower."

I turn around again. I've never been on display like this before. Growing up, I preferred being in the chorus over solos. I didn't take drama or dance or anything that involved performing in front of others. I did well enough in PE, but I didn't participate in extracurricular sports. And I have certainly never undressed in front of a man and allowed him to gawk at me.

What have I gotten myself into?

CHAPTER TWENTY-ONE

The vibe here is definitely different than what I was getting back at the Drescott.

Judging by the rise and fall of his chest, his breath is a little uneven. I'm having an effect on him.

"Play with yourself."

His words introduce a new level of awkwardness. As if I wasn't self-conscious enough already, now I've got to put on a show for him? Where do I begin? What should I do?

I rub an arm. I rub the other arm, moving my hand from my wrist toward my shoulder. It's probably as sexy as watching your grandmother knit. I'm guessing he thinks so, too, because he starts to direct me.

"Caress your neck."

I put my hand to the back of my neck and give myself a little massage, trying to relax myself. I hear a scream in the background. It's probably the woman who's shackled to the floor. I wonder if there are other couples around.

"Now your shoulders."

I wrap myself in an embrace, keeping my eyes averted from him.

"Caress your tits."

I drop my hands to cup my breasts.

"Pull the cups down."

I do as told. I reveal my breasts and notice my nipples have hardened. He shifts against the table

"Feel yourself up."

I think about the woman shackled to the floor and how at ease she seemed spread-eagled and naked in front of her partner. Maybe they've been together a while. Or maybe she's like Sierra, confident in her body.

"Show me how much you love touching yourself."

I massage my breasts.

"Do it like you mean it."

I grope myself more deeply.

"Pinch your nipples."

I follow his instructions.

"Harder."

I pinch them harder. I wonder if I could handle the caning that woman received. Probably not, but a small part of me is curious to try.

"Did you like how that felt?"

Not particularly, but I don't think that's the answer he's looking for, so I say, "Yes, Sir."

The words fall naturally from my lips, surprising both of us. A small smile hovers over his mouth.

"Good. Pinch them even harder then."

I make myself gasp when I do as he bids.

"Mess up your hair."

I shake my hand through my hair.

"Suck on a finger."

I stick a forefinger into my mouth

"Put another finger in."

I'm his personal, live porn show. And it's kind of...titillating. I insert my middle finger.

"Suck them well."

I suck my digits and start to get a little creative, rolling my fingers around my mouth, pulling them in and out as if I'm going down on his cock. I think I hear him groan.

"Rub your fingers on your nipple."

In doing so, I transfer my spit to the nipple, which stretches as hard as it can.

"Now put your hand in your panties and get yourself nice and wet."

God Almighty. As my hand slips into my underwear, I feel so naughty. I worry that I'm too embarrassed to get wet, but there's already moisture there. Maybe it's from before. I circle a finger on my clit.

"Make it feel good for yourself."

I close my eyes and try to block out the fact that I'm in a BDSM club, that he's staring at my every move, that I'm feeling myself up in front of a man I barely know. Instead, I focus on the friction of my finger against my clit. Pleasure begins to build as I stroke myself. Maybe I can do this after all.

"Is this how you pleasure yourself when no one is

looking?"

"Yes. Sir."

"Do you ever finger-fuck yourself?"

I shake my head.

"Do you use a vibrator?"

"I don't have one."

"Why not?"

"Never got around to buying one."

"How often do you masturbate?"

"I'm not sure. I've never kept track."

"Once a day?"

I shake my head and draw some of my moisture over my clit.

"Once a week?"

"Depends on the week. Sometimes it's a couple times, sometimes none. It mostly depends on how busy I am."

He watches me fondle myself for several minutes before asking, "Have you ever used a vibrator on yourself?"

"No, Sir."

He gets off the table and walks over to the chest of drawers. After opening a few, he finds what is looking for: a small black vibrator not unlike the one my roommate sometimes leaves lying around her bed. Walking over, he hands it to me.

"Use it. Make yourself come for me."

My first time with a sex toy and it's going to be in front of him instead of the privacy of my bedroom. I swallow and turn the vibrator on. My fingers tingle. It's rather strong for something barely larger than three AA batteries. It has several bumps on one end and fits easily into my panties. I gasp loudly when it touches my clit. I feel like I'm getting tickled to death there. The sensations are surprisingly potent, stronger, more concentrated than my finger. It's too much. I move it off of me.

"We can be here all night, but you will come for me, Virginia."

I melt at the sound of my name. Bracing myself, I return the vibrator to my clit. I wriggle and squirm as if the vibrations have entered my body and are trying to find a way out. After several seconds, I can't take it anymore. How do women get used to these things? I'm about to offer to return to masturbating myself with my finger when he shoves his hand into my underwear. Grabbing my hand, he presses the vibrator to my clit. He wraps his other arm around my back, and there's no escape. I cry out as I writhe against him.

Holy shit, holy shit.

My clit feels like it's getting attacked, but somehow my body likes it, and instead of the gradual climb toward my orgasm, I am shot out of a cannon. The vibrations at my clit explode through my whole body. I scream so loud I bet everyone in the building can hear, but I have no control. I spasm against Tony.

Right after I hit my climax, my clit can't take anymore. I strain and shake my head vigorously because I can't form the words to tell him to take the vibrator away. *Dear God, please take the vibrator away.*

I nearly sob with relief when he finally does. Switching off the vibrator, he catches me before I crumble to the ground. Sweeping me into his arms, he carries me over to the mattress and lays me down. My clit still pulsing madly, I stare up at the ceiling. Holy crap. I need to get myself a vibrator.

"Thank you, Sir," I say with genuine appreciation.

"And that was the weakest one. Wait till we try something more powerful."

CHAPTER TWENTY-TWO

As amazing as that just felt, I don't think I can take something more powerful.

Setting the vibrator down on the mattress beside me, Tony heads back to the dresser and pulls out a coil of rope. Kneeling on the mattress, he flips me over roughly, in sharp contrast to the gentle way he carried and laid me down. He pulls me to my knees so my ass is in the air. It's a familiar position, only this mattress is not nearly as soft as the one at the Drescott. He yanks my arms toward my butt and ties my wrists behind my thighs. Pulling my panties down, he exposes my buttocks, which he tenderly caresses before giving one a good hard slap. I've never been spanked before. I can't decide if it's humiliating or a turn-on.

It's both.

"Do you remember your safety word?"

"Yes, sir."

"What is it?"

"Tar Heel."

I hope to God I won't have to use it. He reaches between my thighs and caresses me until I'm moaning.

"You got yourself nice and wet."

I love the way he touches me. My body has a way of responding to his every stroke. Despite having had a killer orgasm, my arousal begins anew. As awesome as the vibrator is, I want to come on his hand. My body ties itself in a knot for him. Please make me come.

But he stops his caresses. Maybe to undress himself. Instead, he stands up and makes a phone call on his cell. He's having a full on conversation in French while I'm bent over with my naked butt in the air, wetness trickling down my thighs, pulsing for his attention.

Part way through his call, he leans down and rubs me between my legs and plays with my clit. A whimper escapes my lips but I try to keep quiet, hoping the person on the other line didn't hear anything. Though it's possible Tony has already relayed that he's feeling up some naked American girl right now. He finishes his call just in time to pick up an incoming call

"I'm still in the city," he says as he wanders over to the armoire display case. "I'll be back after dinner."

I think it's Eric he's talking to. I see Tony glance my way.

"I may be a while."

I'm not sure if that's good or bad.

"Tomorrow is fine, but I want to see if my cousin

Ben can join us."

His next call is in Chinese, I assume, and I marvel at how easily he goes from one language to the next. After hanging up, Tony returns to me. Thank goodness. I'm done with being in this awkward hogtie. But he doesn't untie me and instead caresses the contours of my rump, lightly slapping a cheek. I moan when his hand reaches beneath my derrière and strokes my wet folds. He fondles my clit, which has been starving for his touch. Okay, if he's going to keep doing that, I'll stay in this position. His touch feels so good. It doesn't take my arousal long to go from a simmer to a boil.

He has me hot and bothered, my body starting to strain toward release, before stopping. I watch as he walks back to the display case.

"What would you like to try?" he asks, studying the implements inside the case.

I have no idea. They all look intimidating.

"What's best for a beginner?" I ask.

He rubs his thumb along his jaw. "That depends. Do you like stinging or thudding sensations?"

Probably neither, but I reply, "I don't know."

Opening the case, he pulls out a crop and tests it, smacking it into his palm and against his leg, then situates himself behind me. "We will try stinging first."

I tense. This is it. My first real experience with BDSM.

"Relax," he says as he caresses a buttock. "I'll try to go easy."

Try?!

I do have my safety word, but crap, I'm putting a lot of trust in this person. I scold my libido for putting me in this situation.

He taps the end of the crop to my ass. The gentle smacks are almost like a massage, warming my flesh, and in between my legs, I'm a furnace of desire. He raps the crop all over my rump, and just as I start to relax, he whacks me a little harder. I yelp, but it's mostly in surprise. The sting fades quickly. He slaps my other buttock a little harder, but it's still quite tolerable. He glances at my face before returning his attention to my backside. The crop gently kisses my ass several more times before landing harder. This time I cry out at the sting, but the pain doesn't linger. So far the fear has been harder to take than the actual impact of the crop.

But I change my mind on the next blow. This one bites into my ass, leaving me breathless.

He puts his hand on the arch of my derrière. "Stay still. I don't want the crop to land in the wrong place."

The next few smacks are the hardest yet. I cry out at each one, and the stinging doesn't dissipate as quickly as before. The tingling of my skin turns into a burning sensation.

"How are we doing, Virginia?"

"Good."

Maybe I shouldn't have said that for it turns into an invitation to spank me harder. One of the strikes brings tears to my eyes. I start thinking about my safety word.

"You're doing great," he says, pausing to caress the need still pulsing between my legs, building the agitation and making me feel like I'll happily endure more of the crop if he will just make me come.

A minute or so later, he returns to hitting me with the crop. It's getting more challenging keeping my ass in the air for the sole purpose of receiving pain. But I don't want to come across wimpy. I don't want him to regret spending more time with me. So even though I feel like I'm getting poked by hundreds of needles each time the crop falls, I refrain from using my safety word. Plus, when he fondles me, the pain recedes in favor of lust. I moan in pleasure as he plays with my clit.

"You want me to make you come, don't you?" he asks.

I murmur, "Yes, Sir."

"That will be your reward for doing such a good job."

He leaves to put the crop in a basket by the doorway. I'm thinking that's where the used implements go, hopefully to be cleaned before their next use.

"Now for the thudding."

I wonder which items deliver thuds over stings. They all seem like they're capable of both.

He spots my textbook. "This will do."

Oh my God. I never would've thought economics could be used for *this*.

He kneels behind me, and there are no gentle taps this time.

Whack!

My body is driven into the mattress, taking away my breath. Whereas the sting of the crop made me feel as if my skin might crack open, the textbook feels like it will give me bruises. I'm not sure which is worse.

Whack!

I feel the blow all the way from my ass to my head. I'm never going to be able to look at my textbook the same way again. How am I going to read about supply and demand curves now?

"Stay still," Tony reminds me when my body wavers.

He delivers another teeth-jarring blow. Why did I agree to do this?

He answers my question when he touches me, tenderly caressing my burning, aching rump. His fingers return to working their magic. While he strokes my clit, he sinks his thumb into my slit. I'm still a little sore there, but it feels like my clit is being pleasured on both sides, inside and out. I start to tremble. The pain starts blurring with the pleasure, which is much more intense than the masturbation he performed on me at the Drescott. I pray he doesn't stop until I climax.

"Is there something you need to ask me?" he prompts.

Question? What the hell is he talking about?

He withdraws his hand.

No! Don't do that. I can do this. Question. He wants a question. I try not to panic.

And then it dawns on me.

"Can I come, Sir?"

He wallops me with the textbook. "That's to help you remember."

"Thank you, Sir."

"You can come."

When he returns to fondling me, I murmur another, "Thank you, Sir."

My orgasm swirls inside me, ready to burst, mixing pain and pleasure. And when I come, I'm riding a new and beautiful high. I'm like a surfer catching a wave, not the quaint Atlantic ones, but the larger Pacific kind. It washes over me, trembling my body. My limbs would probably be flailing if they weren't bound.

When I finally wash up on the beach, a long and contented sigh escapes me. I wallow in the bliss until the discomfort of my position and the pain in my rear return to my awareness. The blood pulses strongly between my thighs, reminding me it was all worth it.

I want to stretch out or fall onto the mattress, but Tony isn't done.

CHAPTER TWENTY-THREE

I hear him unzip his pants and sense him kneeling behind me. Craning my head, I see him take off his shirt. He must have brought along one of the condoms, which he opens. After putting it on, he rubs his cock along my folds. I find myself eager for him. He's given me two amazing orgasms, I want him to get his.

"You should see how beautiful your ass is right now," he says as the runs his thumb where the crop had stung the most. "Do you bruise easily?"

"I don't think so," I answer, but it may be a while before I'll want to sit down.

His thumb comes close to my anus, and I jump.

"Not ready to lose your last virginity?" he asks.

"Definitely not," I reply.

He murmurs, "I may make you change your mind about that."

My heart skips a beat. I'm not ready for anal sex. It just sounds so wrong. And I don't see how it can be pleasurable. As much as Tony turns me on, I don't know that I will ever want to do it with anyone.

Again I'm cognizant of the helpless position I've

put myself in. If he wanted to penetrate me there, I wouldn't be able to stop him. He's right: selling my virginity this way was dumb.

But when his cock strokes my clit, I feel my IQ dropping. My body has become a glutton for orgasms. At the moment, however, I would be happy just to feel him inside me.

I push myself against his cock. He obliges and pushes a few inches into me. My pussy gleefully takes him in, though it hasn't healed from the previous stretching. He rubs my lower back before sinking further in. I gasp at how hard and large he feels. He rests inside me, grunting when my muscles involuntarily flex about his shaft. Though my pussy is still raw, I savor how he fills me.

"What is your safety word?"

Why is he asking me that? What is he planning on doing?

"Tar Heel," I answer.

He pulls out a few inches, then sinks back in.

"Did you like the crop?"

I hesitate, then say, "Yes."

"Is that the truth? You must not lie to me."

"I liked that I got to come after it was all done."

He keeps his thrusting to small, slow movements, as if acclimating me to him while finding the angle that makes me go weak in the knees.

"Did you like being spanked with your textbook?"

"Honestly? I would have preferred something else

just 'cause...it's a textbook, not a BDSM thing."

"You'd be surprised what can be used for BDSM."

He pushes himself deeper, then reaches for the vibrator, which he turns on and holds to my clit.

Oh. My. God.

The combination of the stimulation to my clit and the sensation of being stretched by his cock is other worldly. My arousal is doing the happy dance. Actually, it's not just happy. It's *ecstatic.*

I gasp. I moan. I whine.

I can't believe I whined, but my control over my body is tenuous. I no longer feel how my shoulders and neck are sore, how my lower body is cramped. All that I feel is his hardness buried inside me and the vibrations jammed up against my clit.

His body cages me, and I bump against his chest. I want to drown in him, drown in the amazing sensations he's wrecking me with, the climax he's building for me.

But it's not easy with Tony. He turns off the vibrator. After a few languid thrusts, he asks again for my safety word.

"Tar Heel," I repeat.

He slams into me so hard I think I feel the concrete beneath the mattress. Over and over his pelvis slaps my sore bottom, reminding me of every strike of the crop, every smack of the textbook. I feel the drilling in my entire body, not just my pussy. After thrusting fast and furious, he gives me a reprieve and brushes aside the hair that has fallen over my face. I gulp, still semi-stunned at the throttling I just received.

He changes up the motion, opting for a deep hard shove, followed by a slow withdrawal, then another deep hard shove. I whimper in between the pounding, but I refrain from using the safety word. I think it will please him if I don't. I opened the door to all this, and I am not going to retreat.

He accelerates his thrusting, holding my hips so that he can go as deep as possible. After getting banged like this—I wonder if this is how it feels to get sacked in football, only football players have the benefit of padding—I start to crumble. The safety word is on the tip of my tongue.

Tony's grunts turn into a roar. He bucks his hips ferociously before slowing down considerably. I can't remember feeling so relieved. He came. Which means he's done.

Hopefully. I think I can never be sure what to expected with Tony.

After a few more pumps, he pulls out and unties my wrists. Even though I desperately want out of my position, it hurts to stretch myself out. I collapse onto the mattress, my body feeling bruised on the inside. Tony wasn't just trying to fuck me hard. It felt like he was trying to fucking kill me.

I hear the vibrator turn on. Part of me doesn't want to feel anything. My body just needs to recover. But after a minute or two of the vibrations, I become receptive, then more than receptive. The vibrator still takes a little getting used to, but the stimulation has my arousal back to where it left off before he started pounding me into oblivion. I cry out as the orgasm bursts within me. As before, my clit quickly becomes overly sensitive, and I grab his hand with both of mine to push the vibrator away, but he keeps me in that head-rattling space for several seconds longer before easing the vibrator away.

Laying there, I feel like I might never be able to get up. I can't believe what my body has just been through. Something more painful than running several miles when I'm one of the worst runners in my class, yet more thrilling than a roller coaster and waking up on Christmas morning.

"Was I too hard?" Tony asks as he lays beside me.

"Yes," I say meekly.

"Why didn't you use your safety word?"

"I didn't want to."

He eyes me with what looks like wonder. I turn my head and meet his gaze. The words are out of my mouth before I can deliberate their wisdom.

"I'd do it again."

Laying back, he stares at the ceiling. "Don't tempt me, *ma petite*."

CHAPTER TWENTY-FOUR

"Does this mean I get to finish out the week?" I ask when we're in the car driving back to Marin County.

"I haven't decided," Tony responds. "You'll get your money either way."

I've made it known that I'm okay with sticking to the terms of the contract, so I don't belabor the point. I'm just glad that he's going to keep me a while longer. I wiggle a little in my car seat, stoking the rawness of my ass to remind myself of what I've been through. Tony had applied a balm to my bottom to cool the skin and help it heal. Even though I cleaned myself at The Lair, the wetness is still dripping, and I don't like having to sit in moist undies. I'm also a lot more sore between the legs.

But it was all worth it. God Almighty was it worth it.

"I don't have to call you 'Sir' in front of Eric and Sierra, do I?" I suddenly wonder.

"That wasn't one of my rules," he replies with half a grin. "That was all you."

Realizing that's true, I blush. "So, are you a long-time practitioner of BDSM?"

"What do you consider a long time?"

"I don't know. Over a few years?"

"Then yes. I started when I was about seventeen."

"Is that when you lost your virginity?"

"Not long after."

I wonder what it would be like to lose one's virginity as a teenager, in high school.

"How did you get into it?" I ask.

"I have cousins who were into hentai. They especially liked porn featuring kinbaku."

I think about Christian Grey's background. "Did you have a special instructor?"

"My subs were my best instructors, but in terms of technique, I learned a lot from my cousin Shen. He used to go to school in this area. Stanford."

"Is he still here? In California?"

Tony seems to stare off into the distance, somewhere beyond the highway. "I don't think so."

I get the feeling this cousin of his is a sensitive topic, so I veer the conversation elsewhere. "Has your family always been in the hotel business?"

"We've owned residential dwellings for centuries."

"Do you like it? The hospitality industry?"

"Do *you* like it?"

"It's a job. I'm not looking to be a hotel maid for the rest of my life."

He chuckled. "If you could be anything, if you didn't have to worry about money or what it takes to get there, what would you be?"

I think for a moment. "I'd still want to do something in social work."

"You don't want to do something more glamorous? Become a singer or movie star?"

"Social work is meaningful to me. You won't make a ton of money or change the world, but you can change someone's life, like Lila did for me."

"That's it? No other ambition?"

Maybe he thinks a career in social work is boring. "Do I need to have other ambitions?"

He looks over at me, appraising. "Most people I know aspire to money or power. And lots of it. They don't seek *meaning*."

"That's kind of sad. What do you aspire to?"

For a second he seems befuddled, as if no one's ever asked him that before.

"I have more money than I know what to do with. And money is power. So on those fronts, I'm done."

"And meaning? Is that something you feel you want?"

"I'm not like you, Virginia. I'm a selfish bastard. I don't have a lot of redeeming qualities. The world would probably be better off without me."

"That's a harsh thing to say about yourself."

"It's the truth. I don't romanticize my existence."

"Even so, you're more than you give yourself credit for."

"You think I fucked you because you wanted it? *La merde*. I fucked you because *I* wanted it. And I fucked you the way I wanted to fuck you. You can't pretend you liked it. I know it hurt."

I look down at my lap, then up again. "But you almost didn't. You wanted to take me home. I'm the one that convinced you otherwise. You can't take all the blame."

He frowns, and I feel as if I've said something else, something other than what I actually said or meant.

"And if I were a good person, you'd be back home instead of in this car. But like I said, I'm a selfish bastard. A part of me just wants you for a fuck toy and not care what it does to you."

I want to gulp but can't. After I find my voice, I ask, "What does the other part want?"

He continues to stare ahead. "Maybe there's no other part."

It seems wrong, but I think I might be okay with that. Am I so starved for a guy's desire such that I'm willing to be devalued into a sex object? Is my self-esteem that low? Or is it the fact that it's wrong that makes it intriguing? I know I'm not okay with being a sex object for just anyone. In fact, I balk at the idea. But with Tony...I find it arousing.

For now. I may think differently, a whole lot differently, later.

We drive in silence for a while till I remember that I should give Talia the heads up that I might not be home tonight or she'll wonder. I take out my phone to text her.

"What app is that?" Tony asks.

"It's this new thing called BW2T, Better Way 2 Text. You can integrate it with a whole bunch of other social apps and create your own emojis. Plus, it has a huge selection of gifs. It's supposed to make texting more fun."

When the car pulls up in front of Eric's place, I'm disappointed. I want Tony to myself.

"Changed your mind?" Eric asks Tony with raised brows when he sees us both.

"Yes," was all Tony said, sounding slightly annoyed with the question.

"We had dinner already, but there's probably leftovers in the kitchen."

Tony turns to me, but I reply that I'm not hungry. I take my duffel bag and textbook upstairs back to the room I had the first night. At least now that I have my textbook, I can study. I'll miss Mr. Parker's office hours, but maybe there's a computer or tablet I can borrow to download the class notes.

"So how'd you get Tony to change his mind?" Sierra asks, leaning against the doorway with her arms crossed in front of her.

"Pretty much begged him," I reply, surprising myself with my retort. Usually I'm stumped and can never think of a comeback.

Sierra snickers. "So he felt sorry for the little redneck."

Refusing to take the bait, I don't answer.

"So how come you guys were gone so long?" Sierra asks.

"We went for a late lunch, early dinner thing," I reply, then ask her so she doesn't probe too much, "What did you and Eric do?"

"Hung out in the hot tub. Had drinks. Sex. What did you think we were doing? Watching a stuffy historical documentary on PBS?"

That girl needs some courtesy slapped into her, I imagine Lila saying. And Lila would do just that if she could be certain she wouldn't land in jail for it. The thought amuses me and dissolves my irritation towards Sierra.

I pick up my textbook and open it, hoping she gets the message, but it backfires.

"I wonder what Mrs. Ruiz or Mr. Danforth would say if they knew you were fraternizing with a guest," Sierra says. "And not just *any* guest."

The Montclair has strict guidelines about employee interactions with hotel guests. I'd probably get fired. And I can't afford to be without a job right now.

"Hopefully they don't find out," I reply, meeting her gaze. The only way they would find out is if Sierra tells them. Or Tony. But he doesn't seem likely to.

"Yeah," was all Sierra said.

I return to my textbook with better luck this time. Sierra walks away. I wish we could get along, and part of me wants to say something to that effect, but I don't think she's looking to be my friend. Kumbaya moments with people like her happen in kid movies, not so much in real life.

But maybe I should give her more of a chance?

Unable to concentrate on price elasticity, especially since I keep thinking about how I was spanked with this book back to The Lair, I decide to change and go downstairs and see what everyone else is doing. Eric and Tony are down in the bachelor room.

"This resort is going to rival Half Moon Bay for sure," Eric is telling Tony as he cycles through television channels with the remote. "Maybe even Monterey."

Tony is sitting in a sofa opposite Eric, smoking a cigar. "Isn't Pebble Beach there?"

"Yeah, but you got to have aspirations. My dad is known for developing some of the world's best golf courses. If anyone can give Pebble Beach a run for its money, it's us. All we need are some visionary investors."

"Like the Lee family."

"Exactly. Since you guys have a lot of hotel experience, we might even let you advise us on that piece."

Seeing me, Tony puts out the cigar. I feel a tiny bit guilty that he's cutting short his smoking. But it's better for him.

"Don't mind me," I say as I walk toward the billiard table. "I was just going to shoot some pool."

Eric spares me a glance, then goes back to talking to Tony. "Your family should stick to development. Forget all that tech investment. This resort I'm developing is going to return so much more for your family if you get in on the ground floor."

"Undertaking large development projects in California isn't easy from what I've heard."

Eric puts down his glass of bourbon and helps himself to a cigar. "Which is why we're not doing it in near the Bay Area where liberal politicians are going to make us jump through hoops convincing them that our project isn't going to damage the environment or force us to sign fucked-up project labor agreements."

"Aren't project labor agreements about living wages?" I venture. I know next to nothing about real estate development, but it just so happens I read an article in the newspaper last week about some housing project being delayed over project labor agreements.

Eric looks at me, then back to Tony. "You picked a crazy one."

Tony turns to me. "Living wages is a major reason a politician would support PLA's."

I nod a thank you for answering my question, then look at the balls on the table. I've only played pool a few times, and these balls are not the multicolored ones I've seen before. The balls look smaller and are most are red.

"No," objects Eric. "Democrats support PLA's because they want to shore up their base of support among the unions. And because they're fucking communists."

Tony gets up and walks over to where I'm standing. He picks out a cue stick.

As if worried that he might have offended Tony, Eric quickly follows with, "Your family's not what I would consider communist. If you didn't embrace capitalism, you wouldn't have made the kind of money you did. I heard that your family didn't lose all its property to Ho Chi Minh because of its triad connections."

Tony doesn't say anything and passes balls my way, sliding them across the table.

"I understand one of your family members is the head of the *Jing San Triad*."

Tony tells me to rack the balls. I start sticking a bunch of them into the triangle.

"How close are you and your brother to that part of the family?"

Tony comes up next to me and pulls out the non-red balls inside the triangle. I can smell the cigar on him, which isn't my favorite, but my pulse skips a beat at his nearness.

Eric takes a puff of his cigar, his gaze keenly on Tony. "What's it like to kill a man?"

CHAPTER TWENTY-FIVE

I remove the triangle, but Eric's question jars me, and I knock several balls out of place. I look over at Tony, whose jaw tightens. Is Eric asking for real?

"You did a lot of this 'opposition research,'" Tony notes.

Eric grins. "We know the dirt on all our business partners."

"And, as with your political opponents, you're not afraid to use the dirt."

I stare at Tony. He hasn't refuted Eric's question.

Eric holds up his hands. "Look, I don't hold it against your family."

"You shouldn't. Your family has its share of shady dealings."

Eric looks surprised. "Yeah, well, our lawyers say we're covered. You don't have to worry about any of that, especially when we're on the same team. If you ask me, the mafias know how to run business. There's the godfather, the CEO, that everyone listens to. We'd get so much more shit done in this country if our government was run the same way. So the dude you killed, was he a rival triad member?"

My eyes widen. Tony turns to me.

"My cousin, May, and I were ambushed in Hanoi," he explains as he continues to look at me. "I was cleared by the court as having acted in self-defense."

Eric leans over the sofa with rapt interest. "Was it really just self-defense?"

Tony narrows his eyes at Eric. "What are you suggesting?"

"After watching *The Godfather* movies—best flicks of all time, though *Goodfellas* is a pretty close second—I've wondered if I could ever kill someone. If I had to, you know, because that's what happens when you're part of the mafia. My father was approached by the mafia once, decades ago, about a business deal, but my dad wanted to go it alone. When you're as rich as us, who needs the mafia?"

I can't quite believe the words that are coming out of Eric's mouth except that it's overshadowed by the revelation that Tony killed a man. How involved is he with criminal elements? Somehow I'm not as surprised as I should be. The wariness I felt when I first met Tony returns double.

Before I can form a question, Sierra prances into the room holding a tray. "Guess what I made today—Jell-o shots!"

She's changed outfits and is now wearing a crop top, shorts that allow her butt cheeks to peek out of the bottom, and platform sandals. Compared to her, I must look frumpy in my sweats, t-shirt and flip flops.

Eric's eyes light up. "Sweet!"

She plops down next to Eric on the sofa and puts the tray on the coffee table.

"What did you use?" Eric asks.

"Your best bottle of vodka." She takes a puff on his cigar.

"You ever try a Jell-o shot?" Eric asks Tony.

Tony eyes the jiggling globs with skepticism, "I prefer my vodka straight—without lots of sugar and...green-ness."

Eric slurps down a shot. "You're missin' out. Man, I don't think I would have made it through college without these babies."

"Maybe it would be more appetizing taking it off my body," Sierra offers, pulling off her top to reveal a lacy balconette bra.

"Hell yeah!"

She shimmies out of her shorts and lays over the coffee table in her lacy thong underwear. Eric plops several shots on her midsection. I turn away and watch Tony place the non-red balls in various places on the table.

"What is this game?" I ask. What I want to ask is about what happened in Hanoi, but I doubt he wants prying questions from someone he barely knows.

"This is a snooker table," he explains.

No wonder this all looked unfamiliar.

"I don't know how to play."

He hands me a cue and chalk. "The goal is to score more points than your opponent. You can go first and break the balls, but don't try to spread too many of them all over the table the way you would in pool. Because if you do and you miss, you give me more balls to sink."

I do as he instructs and dislodge three red balls, but my mind is only partially on the game.

"Red balls are worth one point each," he tells me, "and you have to sink a red one before you can attempt a colored ball worth more points."

Sierra giggles loudly. I feel isolated with Tony in our corner of the room. Well, we're just playing a billiard game. Nothing dangerous about that. I aim the cue ball at a red ball closest to a pocket.

"Hold the cue further back." He takes my hand and repositions it closer to the bottom. "You'll have more control and extension holding it back here."

"Thanks," I say. His touch sends flutters through me, either because I'm nervous or because I'm back to being a teenage girl crushing for the first time. I force myself to focus on the game and surprise myself when the target ball falls into the pocket.

"Now you can aim for the yellow ball, which is worth two points."

I walk over to the other side of the table where the cue ball has come to rest and lean down to view the target. He walks over and, placing his hand on my back, presses me lower. My breath skitters.

"Try to sight the ball at the level of the table," he advises, his hand resting on my back longer than necessary. "And make sure you follow through on your shot."

I nod and surprise myself again when the yellow ball rolls into the pocket. Only the cue ball does, too.

"Too much top spin," he explains, retrieving the yellow ball and placing it back in its original spot.

"I didn't mean to give it top spin," I say as he takes out the cue ball. "That didn't happen the first time."

"Your cue struck the ball above center."

He sets the cue ball on the table, aims for a red ball and sinks it. The cue ball comes to a rest perfectly in line for him to sink the green ball, which he does, followed by another red ball.

"I think I know who's going to win this game," I say.

From the corners of my eyes, I see Eric pull down Sierra's bra cup and put a shot of Jell-o over her nipples. With his mouth, he envelopes the shot and her nipple.

The brown ball misses the pocket by less than an inch, and it's my turn again. I select the red ball I think is the easiest target and lower myself over the table.

"So I should avoid hitting it too high if I don't

want it to spin forward?" I ask.

Tony leans his cue against the table. Hovering over me, he puts each of his hands on one of mine. I feel his chest against my back, his body heat wrapping me. How the heck am I supposed to concentrate now?

"Make sure your bridge doesn't move," he says, pressing my left hand firmly to the table. With his other hand over my right, he manipulates the cue, putting the tip at different parts of the cue ball. "Hit below and you'll get back spin. Hit here and the cue ball will spin right after striking the target. This side will take it left. And if you wanted top spin, you would hit the ball higher."

He backs away to let me take the shot. Although his nearness excites me, it's better that he doesn't discompose me. I hit the cue ball the way I want, and the red ball rolls into the pocket. I glance at Tony with a smile. He returns my smile, looking relaxed. In that moment, he doesn't seem nefarious at all. He killed a man in self-defense. If that wasn't true, he'd be in jail right now. I don't know why I question any of it. I look over the table for my next target.

"Survey the entire table," Tony tells me. "You'll get a better sense of the possibilities that way."

After looking over my options, I choose to go for the blue ball. I miss terribly because just as I move the cue, Sierra emits a shriek and giggle. Eric is lapping bits of broken Jell-o off her breast.

Now it's Tony's turn, and he knocks off six balls in row. In the meantime, Eric and Sierra have started making out.

"You ever think about becoming a professional snooker player?" I ask.

He shakes his head and successfully sinks another red ball.

"What else do you enjoy doing?"

He applies more chalk to his cue. "I think you have a sense of what else I enjoy doing."

I feel my face redden. "Do you...like to travel? Read? Watch movies?"

"What do you like to do?"

"I like going to Andre's basketball games. When Mo was alive, I loved hanging out in the backyard whenever he fired up the grill. I think I might like to travel someday. Maybe see what pho tastes like in Vietnam."

"Hope you guys didn't want any of the Jell-o shots," Eric calls to us, "'Cause we finished 'em all."

Sierra tosses her hair and giggles. "Let's do the hot tub. But I'm going to need something cold to drink. You got any expensive beer?"

Eric grabs bottles from the fridge, and the two of them stumble toward the patio doors.

"You must read," I say to Tony. "You knew about *Fifty Shades Darker*. What else do you like to read? For fun."

It intrigues me that he reads and makes him seem less...criminal. My impression of men is that they don't read that much, and if they do, it's usually the *Wall Street Journal* or *Sports Illustrated*.

Tony leans across the table and aims for the yellow ball. "I do not have many hours for pleasure reading these days, but when I was younger, I read Arsan, Réage, and de Sade."

I don't know the first two names, but I shouldn't be surprised by the last one.

"Are they any good?" I ask.

Tony steps up to me, invading my space. He has that look in his eyes, and I wonder if I'm in trouble. "Only read de Sade if you're ready to see the darker side of humanity. Or your own."

"I guess I'll stick to *Fifty Shades*. For now."

He cups my jaw and draws me to him, his gaze searing mine. "Bad enough you crossed my path."

My heart beats twice as fast as before.

Run away.

But part of me wants to be even closer to him. I don't understand why I'm drawn to someone that unsettles me as much as he does.

Abruptly, he releases my jaw. "Your turn."

Too rattled, I fail to pocket a red ball.

He runs the table till there's only a red ball and a black ball left. Sierra comes in, still in her underwear but dripping wet from being in the hot tub. She grabs two bottles of ale from the fridge before heading back outside.

I look at where the balls are, and if I can pocket the red ball, the black ball is sitting within easy shot of the corner pocket. I get the feeling Tony left the setup for me on purpose.

"You win regardless of whether I get these balls in or not," I say.

The cue ball is in the center of the table, and I have to stretch my body to reach it. My breath catches when Tony leans over me, his mouth an inch from my ear.

"Then how about I give you an incentive?" he asks. "Pot the balls and you win. If I win, I get to spank you with the cue."

I lose focus on the cue ball as I consider how heavy and hard the cue stick is. I don't think it would feel good on my bottom at all.

"That's okay," I say with a shaky laugh.

"Virginia, you don't have a choice."

I was afraid of that. He moves away to give me space to make my shot. I stare hard at the cue ball. I visualize it going in. I need it to go in.

Drawing back the cue, I bring it forward, hitting the cue ball. After rolling about two feet, it hits the red ball

CHAPTER TWENTY-SIX

The red ball teeters at the edge of the pocket. I can't believe I didn't hit it hard enough.

A second later the ball falls into the pocket, and I jump with excitement. I look over at Tony.

"Nice shot," he says, "but you still have to pot the black ball."

Feeling like a soldier going into battle, I nod and brace myself. Based on where the cue ball ended up, I can't hit the target ball straight on. It's resting near the rail. I could try to ricochet the ball off the rail, but that leaves room for a lot of error, and I'm not skilled enough to attempt that.

Tony goes to stand behind the black ball and points to the side of it. "You want the cue ball to gently kiss the black ball here."

Is he helping me out because he doesn't think I can make this shot or because he's not that vested in spanking me with the cue?

He puts a finger on the bumper just an inch or so to the left of the black ball. "Aim the cue ball right here."

I chalk my cue and position myself over the table.

I don't want to think about how hard the cue is or about the possibility that if Tony hits me really hard, it might even break.

Instead, I visualize the cue ball heading toward his finger and tapping the black ball on its side, and the black ball rolling toward the corner pocket, falling in.

I can do this.

As soon as I hit the cue ball, I worry that I've hit it too softly again. It rolls rather slowly toward the black ball and might not have enough power to send the black ball into the pocket. Tony walks over to me, and together we watch the cue ball hit the spot his finger had been pointing to. The energy transfers to the black ball, which rolls toward the corner of the table. My grip tightens on my cue as I realize I might have done it.

The ball falls into the pocket.

"I did it!" I squeal and turn around to face Tony.

His eyes seem to reflect my delight as he wraps an arm around my waist and pulls me to him.

"Congratulations," he says. "You escaped a brutal spanking."

He's exaggerating, right? Nonetheless, my relief increases. I hadn't wanted to consider what kind of spanking he had intended.

He crushes his mouth over mine, making my head spin. I'm glad I didn't take any of those Jell-o shots so that I can experience his kiss unadulterated by alcohol. It's a high unlike anything I can think of. I feel powerless to stop him from devouring my lips, provided I would want to. Which I don't. I love how strong his mouth feels on mine, yet there's a finesse there. It's not just about pressing lips to lips like some passionate kiss from an old film in a time when actors couldn't kiss with mouths open. I feel like Tony is savoring my mouth while claiming every millimeter of it as his.

Without separating his mouth from mine, he takes my cue from my hand and lays both mine and his on the table. Scooping me, he sits me on the edge of the table and continues to kiss me, probing deeper this time. His hand at the back of my neck alarms me a little, just because it's such a vulnerable place. How had he killed this man in Hanoi anyway?

The question fades as his tongue delves into my mouth. I do my best to respond, but he doesn't leave much room for me to guide the action. Warmth flares through me, stymied only by the fact that Sierra or Eric might walk in on us at any moment. But there's no way I want this to stop. The scent of the cigar doesn't bother me as much as that of cigarettes, and I think I could kiss Tony for hours.

Tentatively, I reach for him. I'm not completely sure if I'm allowed to touch him, but I wrap my hand about his neck the way he does to me. He shoves his tongue harder into my mouth. I can feel the tone of the kiss change. He's been holding back, but his ardor is rising. The unleashing of it is where it might get dangerous. But we're not at The Lair. We're in someone else's place. And we don't have the privacy of Cell Three That should temper what he does. I think.

Abruptly he pulls me off the table, whirls me around, and bends me over the table.

"I thought I escaped the spanking," I protest.

His hand is still on my back, holding me down. "This isn't going to be a spanking. It's a fucking."

What...

He slips his hand easily into my sweats while his body pins me to the table.

"But Eric and..." My words disappear as he starts to rub me. I'm not an exhibitionist. Small public displays of affection are okay, but making out in public is not something I would ever consider doing. Getting fucked where people can see is beyond my comprehension.

Only this is happening. What's worse, my embarrassment if Eric or Sierra should walk in on us isn't dampening my arousal. In fact, it doesn't take long before my I'm wet for him. He rubs my damp underwear against me, and I moan, wanting more. But I don't. At least not here, bent over a snooker table. His fingers slide beneath my underwear and spread my wetness over my flesh.

"Eric and Sierra are right outside the door," I try again.

Just shut up and let him do his thing, my libido tells me.

His fingers have me agitated nice and good, and I feel my hold on propriety slipping. I can't believe I'm letting this happen.

"The patio doors are open. They'll be able to hear."

"What will they hear? Your moans of pleasure? Or are you worried you might scream?"

"All of the above."

He yanks down my sweats and tears my underwear. Before I can ask him anything, my underwear is stuffed into my mouth. I try to take out my underwear, but my wrists are whipped behind my back. This is horrifying. My cum is on my underwear, which is now in my mouth, where it should never be. I think I taste myself.

I feel his hardness through his jeans against my ass. He holds my wrists in place with one hand while his other goes back to fondling me between my thighs. Trapped between him and the table, I feel utterly helpless. I pray that Eric and Sierra stay outside. If they walked in, this would be more than a little humiliating.

"I'm sure they're busy," Tony says.

He's right. I can hear the occasional murmur and grunt from Sierra. Maybe the best way out of my predicament is to get it over with as soon as possible.

No complaints here, my libido says.

I'm gushing between the legs, desire straining for that euphoric end. I'm close. Really close.

But he pulls his hand away. I hear him unzipping and the tearing of foil. After some jostling, his length is between my thighs, gliding along my pussy lips. A little more of that and I'll come. Right against the table. With a wad of cotton underwear stuffed in my mouth.

He slides himself into my slit. I close my eyes and block out Eric and Sierra not twenty feet from us. At least they can't see us from where they are.

My pussy flexes about him. I wonder if he will always feel this hard inside of me, or will my vagina get used to him if he keeps stretching me like this? I emit a shaky groan into my underwear as he slowly begins to thrust. Ardor presses into me, concentrating between my legs, ready to flower. He intensifies the sensation with every withdrawal and every plunge. His motions are long, measured, angled just right. I want to come so badly. Please make me come.

I cry out and quiver as rapture blooms and ripples through me. That I'm pressed against a hard surface, the edge of the table digging into me, my sweats around my knees, does nothing to diminish the beautiful, marvelous bliss that engulfs me.

He sweeps my hair into a ponytail in his free hand and tugs. Hard. I yelp and consider spitting out my underwear, but I need it. He releases my wrists and pulls my hair back while simultaneously shoving himself deep into my pussy. Now his rhythm is fast, his motions short but deep. I brace myself against the surface of the table, trying to push back against him so I don't end up becoming one with the table. If he pounds me any harder, I might break a bone against the snooker table.

The underwear helps to muffle my grunts and cries. The fucking is jarring, and my scalp starts to burn. I realize I won't be able to speak my safety word. Not that I can remember it.

He slows down. Thank God. I grasp the opportunity to take a normal breath. His pace is now more than bearable, and I find my arousal simmering anew. Still holding my hair in one hand, he reaches his other hand around to grope a breast. This gentler fondling is an exciting relief to the ferocity from a moment ago. Adrenaline is pumping through me, magnifying every sensation. I collect myself just in time. He grinds himself deeper into me,

I wonder if he's come because he pulls out of me, but I realize he hasn't when he flips me onto my back. He sinks back in and pulls my wrists above my head, pinning them to the table. He bucks his hips gradually as his gaze locks with mine. Despite the awkward position with my legs dangling over the table, my feet unable to touch the floor, I start to crave another orgasm.

How do you do this to me? I ask through my eyes.

I'm such a mess. My body still feels worn from his earlier fucking, but arousal still rises. The stroking of his cock inside me is exhilarating. I want that high again, and I'll suffer anything to achieve it. If he wants to pound me into a pulp, I'll take it if he can make me feel this good.

Yes, this good. So good. I'm gonna come again.

"Ask permission first," he warns me.

My underwear garbles my words, but surely he knows what I'm trying to say.

"*Pardon.* Say again?" he replies with a mischievous glimmer in his eyes.

I try again but it comes out, "A ah unh, er?"

He continues his tantalizing thrusting, his pelvis pressing into my clit when he penetrates extra deep.

Please. "EEEase."

Worrying that my body can't hold out much longer, I start to beg through my eyes. He seems to note my desperation and says, "You've earned it. Come."

A few more thrusts from him, and I convulse, my back arching off the table. He pumps into me harder and faster till rapture overtakes him, too. After my orgasm subsides, I savor the feel of his body over mine, the pulsing of his cock inside me.

Until I turn my head and see Eric standing at the threshold.

CHAPTER TWENTY-SEVEN

The single user handicap bathroom at my elementary school had a broken lock on it. But one day I had to go really bad and didn't think I wanted to make it all the way to the girls' restroom, so I availed myself of what is nearest. I wasn't done going when Bradley, a boy in the fifth grade I had a crush on, opened the bathroom door.

For days after, I dreaded going to school.

The church picnic was another source of my most embarrassing moments. Somehow the grape punch went down the wrong pipe and I started coughing—right onto Mrs. Johnson, the pastor's wife, spewing purple all over her white linen dress.

Getting caught with my pants down, literally, with my underwear balled in my mouth is right up there.

Tony pulls me to my feet as if nothing could be more normal. My entire face is the color of a fire hydrant as I yank up my sweats and turn away to spit out my underwear.

"Just make sure you clean up any wet spots," Eric snickers as he makes his way to the bar.

"I'm..." I mutter, but I don't bother finishing the

sentence. I turn and head out of the room with quick steps. I would rather be anywhere but here.

Back in my room, I flop face down on the bed and scream into the pillow. Given the late hour, I have nowhere to go. I'm stuck in a house up in the hills of Marin County. With at least two people I'm not thrilled to be hanging out with, and a third whom I am reconsidering whether or not I want to be with. Just because he makes my body go haywire doesn't mean he's worthwhile company.

I take a brief, hot shower, which helps to calm me down. I throw on my pajama shirt and new underwear. As I brush my teeth, I look about the room and see my textbook next to the bed. I shouldn't be here. I should be at work and in class. I don't have much with me, so packing back up wouldn't take long at all.

"I warned you about me."

Whipping around, I see Tony standing at my door. My shame turns to anger toward him. I stomp back into the bathroom to finish brushing my teeth. He follows me and leans against the doorframe.

"You can't tell me you weren't titillated by the prospect that we might get walked in on," he says.

I spit toothpaste into the sink and reply, "I thought the chances of that happening weren't so high."

"Don't take risks if you can't accept the consequences."

"You didn't exactly give me a choice!"

I throw water in my mouth, then spit it out. I clean the toothbrush and try to walk past him, but he grabs my arm.

"Are you mad at me?" he asks.

I'm mad that Eric saw us, and since Tony started it, I am mad at him. I try to pull my arm away, but his grip is hard and tight about me.

"You didn't specifically say that we were going to, you know, where people could see!" I say.

"You didn't specifically complain."

He makes a valid point. And maybe I *was* a little excited that we might get caught in the act. But that was before I realized just how embarrassed I would feel when it actually happened!

"What does it matter that Eric saw us?" Tony presses, still holding onto me. "We're not paying you and Sierra to play patty-cake with us."

My cheeks burn, and for some strange reason I'm a little hurt that he's lumped us in the same category with Sierra and Eric.

"So he saw my cock inside your cunt," Tony continues. "He's a grown man."

"And my underwear stuffed in my mouth!"

His gaze heats, his eyes turning molten. "And it's the sexiest thing he'll ever see."

I flush. If he thinks he can make it all better with a compliment, he's...partially right. When he looks at me like that, I can actually believe he means what he says.

But my indignation won't disappear so easily.

I feel like my dignity is at stake even though I can reason to myself that it shouldn't matter what Eric saw. His imagination could probably conjure worse. And at least he wasn't taking pictures. After this is all over, our paths are unlikely to cross again. He's probably seen a lot more in his days. Who knows, in a few weeks he probably won't even remember. So why should I make such a big deal about it?

And a part of me did like that what Tony and I were doing was naughty. I wasn't raised to like something like this. Well, I'm not sure what I was raised to like about sex. Lila was very matter of fact about it. I remember her telling me that it was okay to feel sexual attraction and that I would know in my heart when it was right. She had no hard and fast rules about sex except that I had to respect myself and demand that my partner respect me, too.

"You want a clear choice?" he asks—no, demands—as he jerked me to him. Grasping my jaw, he keeps my gaze locked with his. "If you choose to stay with me, anything goes. Anything and everything."

Before I can respond, his lips crush mine. I'm not done being angry with him, but I can't escape his hold of me. All I can do is wiggle pathetically against his grasp. I can't protest. His mouth is all-consuming.

What is the matter with me? Why do I let him dominate me like this, and why does my body like it?

He backs me to the wall while his mouth continues to devour me. I offer feeble resistance.

After working my mouth till it is sore, he takes a break, letting me catch my breath and perhaps trying to catch his own. He presses his forehead to mine.

"You up for anything and everything? Can you take it?"

My head is spinning too much to form a coherent thought. I don't usually like confined spaces, but somehow my body enjoys being trapped by his.

The answer is no. You don't want to go there with this guy. You're a newbie when it comes to sex and BDSM. Don't think you can play in his league.

The defiant part of me rejects such condensation. It's the part of me that decided I was going to compete for the fourth grade science fair award because a boy in my class said that boys make better scientists. I didn't end up winning, but I was happy because another girl did.

"What's anything and everything?" I ask, stalling for time.

"Rough sex. Hard sex. Brutal sex."

Hello? How can any of that sound good to you?

But it does. With Tony, it does. Because on the flipside of all that is pleasure that I never imagined my body could experience.

I don't have an answer for him yet. He pulls my shirt over my head but doesn't pull it off my arms. Turning me around, he twists and ties my shirt, locking my arms behind my back. He scoops me in his arms, kicks the bedroom door closed, and deposits me on the bed.

"What are you going to do?" I ask a little nervously. I think I'm always going to be a little nervous around him.

"Help you make up your mind."

He pulls off my underwear. I hope he doesn't stick it in my mouth. As I sit with my knees up, he spreads my legs and swirls his finger over my clit, coaxing the bud to emerge.

"Don't move if you want the bedroom door to stay closed."

He walks into the bathroom and rummages through my toiletry bag. He finds a brand-new toothbrush head, which he uses to replace the one already on my toothbrush. He's going to brush his teeth?

He grabs my toothbrush and the dental floss before returning to the bed. Setting the toothbrush down, he pulls out a long length of floss. What the heck is he going to do with dental hygiene?

He starts winding the floss around my clit. I stare in astonishment. What the...? My clit protrudes like a pink pearl amidst the tied up flesh. He tugs on the floss, and I find myself moaning at the pulling sensation. He tugs up and down, side to side. I moan even more. He takes the other end of the floss, still attached to the plastic container, and loops it around my neck. He ties the floss, which constantly pulls on my clit unless I lean forward, but there's not enough slack in the floss for me to do so comfortably. He walks over to a pot of lilies on the dresser. He plucks off a petal, returns, and gently brushes it over my clit.

It tickles. In a nice, almost unbearable way. When the petal brushes up, I shake and strain. God Almighty. Who thought a little ole flower petal could prove so potent?

"Don't move," he reminds me when my body jerks away at the next kiss of the petal.

I try to stay still, partly because when I do move, I end up tugging on the floss. It's not easy because my body wants to run away from the petal, and yet, I can feel my climax, which I do want, inching closer. And I do not want the door opened. Bad enough Eric saw me with undies in my mouth. But being tortured by dental floss and a flower petal?

My toes curl and my legs quiver as Tony intensifies the brushing. He tweaks a nipple, rolls the other one between his fingers, flicks the former one. It's more sensation than I can take. Wetness is pooling beneath my ass. I'm actually going to come, because of a flower, with dental floss around my clit.

Or not.

He stops brushing me with the petal and leans in to kiss me. I pour all the frustration, tension and relief into the kiss. As if he knows I need this, he lets me, and when I have diffused some of the agitation, he takes over. Clasping the back of my head, he roams over my lips, tastes the inside of my mouth, tugs and sucks my bottom lip until I whimper with need. With his thumb beneath my chin, he tilts my mouth up so that he can press down harder from above.

I realize I'm his to do as he pleases. I let him tie dental floss to my privates for Chrissakes.

His mouth disengages, and his thumb takes the place of where his tongue was. I suck on the digit, conveying my ardor. I want a happy end to all that I've endured.

Picking up the toothbrush, he turns it on and places it on top of my clit.

I shriek. "Holy shit!"

I inadvertently throw my head back, which tugs my clit more fully into the toothbrush. My hapless body doesn't know which direction to run. He takes away the toothbrush. I pant. This is crazy. He's using my toothbrush for a vibrator, and my clit is so sensitive right now, so engorged, that the vibrations are killing me.

"Relax," he says. "You can come whenever you feel like it."

It sounds like a good thing, but I'm not so sure. He puts a hand on one knee to keep my legs from closing together. I squeal through clenched teeth when he applies the toothbrush again. I squirm, and one of my legs folds inward in an attempt to knock his arm away.

He grabs my chin and turns my gaze toward him. "Don't move. You want to come, don't you?"

I stare into his dark eyes and nod.

The toothbrush is back at my clit. I squeeze my eyes shut and try to breathe through the overwhelming sensations. I can do this. I did it with the actual vibrator. I can do it with a toothbrush. I groan and gasp through each reapplication of the toothbrush, simultaneously relieved and disappointed each time he withdraws the toothbrush. Until he doesn't. He places the toothbrush at my most sensitive spot and his finger on the side so that my clit is trapped, vibrating between the bristles and his digit. Within seconds, my orgasm plows into me, and I can't stay still. I almost wish I was completely restricted because I end up pulling too hard on the floss.

He has a tight grip on my thigh, holding me in place as I convulse, trying to scramble away from the toothbrush while euphoria pumps through my veins.

"Please!" I beg. "Oh God, please!"

He releases me and turns off the toothbrush. I fall onto my side, curled in a fetal position, my clit

throbbing like crazy.
    Anything and everything.

CHAPTER TWENTY-EIGHT

He's not done with me.

He takes off his clothes. After he removes the floss and frees my arms from my shirt, I stretch out my limbs, thinning the tension that has collected in my muscles. He lays over me, pressing me face down into the bed. I feel his hardness prod my backside. Anything and everything probably includes anal sex. God Almighty.

Luckily, he aims his cock lower, sinking into my pussy, the entry made easy by the copious amount of wetness there. He murmurs something that sounds like 'zut.' In this position, the depth of penetration is limited, even as he bends his legs, straddling the outside of my thighs, but the angle hits me just right. When I envision sex, I picture the missionary position more often than not. I equate humping from the back with four legged creatures, but I can't deny the pleasure I derive from being taken from behind.

After settling himself more fully inside of me, he brushes aside my hair to kiss my neck and upper shoulders. It feels surprisingly intimate. Contrary to his rougher motions downstairs, he rolls his hips with much more tenderness. I sigh at the gentler approach, content to be caged beneath his weight. Gradually, he tries to leverage off the bed to deepen his thrusts. There's not much I can do except lay there. I can't see him, I can't touch him. Except with my pussy, which flexes about him, making him groan. He entwines his fingers in mine.

My journey to orgasm this time is much less frenetic. I can savor each stroke and relish the slow build-up. It's like taking the scenic route, and when I reach my climax, I'm ready for it. With a cry, I feel like I'm able to ride the wave instead of being wiped out by it. He quickens his pace after I come, his groin slapping faster and more furious against my ass. I feel him spasm against me as he comes. With a loud grunt, he bucks against me a few more times before settling his body over me. I breathe in satisfaction.

I'm exhausted. It's been a marathon of sex, and it hasn't even been twenty-four hours. Can I really take another day of this?

Tony pulls out of me and lays beside me. "So is that a 'yes?'"

I close my eyes. As I fade into slumber, I murmur my response.

Yes.

*****

In the morning, I wake up in the crook of Tony's arm. I'm not sure how I got there, if he reached for me or I imposed myself into his body. But it feels nice. Really nice. I glance at his face to see that he's staring up at the ceiling.

"Awake long?" I ask.

He turns to me. "An hour, maybe an hour and a half."

I start. "Really?"

I like the way his lashes move when his gaze takes in my face from my brow to my lips, and his voice is relaxed when he speaks. "I didn't want to wake you by moving."

"That's, um, nice of you."

He looks away with a snort, rejecting the compliment. "You think it's for your benefit, *ma petite*? I want you rested for anything and everything."

So much for the relaxed moment. I finger the uneven ridge along his pec. "Is this a scar or a birthmark?"

"A scar," he answers with disinterest.

"How'd you get it?"

"A knife wound."

"Is that when you were attacked in Hanoi?"

"Yes."

"That must have been scary. Were you hurt in any

other way?"

"No."

"And your cousin? Was she okay?"

"A few minor bruises. I think the effects afterward were harder for her to bear."

I should probably leave it at that, but curiosity gets the better of me. "Was it for you as well?"

"I was angry. If I hadn't fended off the ambush, May could have been...they wouldn't have killed her, she's worth too much for that. But they could have done other things to her. Auction her off as a sex slave. Make her work on their porn films. The Mao Group engages in a lot of sex trafficking."

"What would they have done to you?"

He laughs. "Ransomed me for sure. Maybe tortured me. One of the Mao Group lieutenants doesn't like me since I beat up his younger brother decades ago."

"Were—are you part of a triad?"

He meets my gaze and can't seem to look away. "I left that life a long time ago."

I mostly believe him. "How were you in it?"

"A different part of my family lives in that world."

"Are you truly able to leave that world?"

"Our family is very practical. I'm worth more out than in. And I was never really that involved. I was just a teenager fucking around, rebelling against my father. But I got my cousin Benjamin into it, and my uncle accused me of ruining his son's future. Our fathers sent us off to boarding schools. Me to Paris. Benjamin to London."

"Benjamin is the one you invited to evaluate Eric's project?"

Tony nods.

"What time are you guys heading up to the site?"

"Eric thought ten o'clock."

I look at the clock. "You should get ready then."

Throwing back the covers, I get out of bed, but Tony yanks me back.

"You've got to take care of something first," he says, pulling aside the bed cover to reveal his hard-on. He pushes my head toward it.

Knowing what he wants, I wrap my mouth about his erection. He murmurs his approval and weaves his fingers through my hair, tugging me down further down his length. I grasp the base of his shaft as I glide my mouth up and down. I'm not sure who's in the position of power here. He's making me give him head, but I want it just as much. I want to make him come. I want to *see* him come, rendered momentarily helpless by his orgasm, knowing I made it happen.

With zest, I suck on him. He tightens his grip on my hair. He lets me work him for several minutes before sitting up. He reaches for his pants, which are on the floor, and retrieves a condom. Unwrapping it, he rolls the condom down his cock. I lick my lips involuntarily. That shaft of his has penetrated the deepest parts of me, been where no one and nothing has been before. Grabbing my leg, he makes me straddle him. He moves me over him, grinding my pussy against his rod. The ease with which he manipulates me makes me feel like I'm five pounds, and my pussy is loving the contact, the friction. Moisture eventually flows down, making my glide smoother along his shaft.

After he's worked me up, roused my craving, has me groaning my pleasure, he lifts me up and settles me over his cock. My vagina hasn't completely healed, but the soreness doesn't bother me. I want this too much. He's so beautiful with his bronzed skin, sculpted body, and black hair. My ardor can't get enough of him, the way he rolls into me, the wave he sets me on. I'm becoming an addict. Maybe I already am.

The percolation in my loins spreads, erupting into tremors as I cry out my release. He bucks his hips in rhythm to my up and down motion, spearing into me just as I descend. My body absorbs the impact, the pain muted by the endorphins rushing through my body. He gaze locks with mine as he comes, shoving hard and deep into me, taking my breath away. He lets go of my hips, and I crumble atop him. I lay there, breathing with the rise and fall of his chest. He rubs the back of my head and even strokes my hair. His cock is still throbbing inside of me.

I realize I like this too much and shift. He grabs

his cock, holding onto the condom so that it doesn't unexpectedly come off.

"I should let you get ready," I say, climbing off him.

"Would you like to come see the project site?"

I try not to look too glad that he's interested in my company.

"Um, sure," I answer.

He goes into the bathroom to toss the condom, then grabs his clothes. "I'll tell Eric. There's probably breakfast down in the kitchen if you're hungry."

After Tony leaves, I ready myself, giddy that I can spend more time with Tony. I even apply a little make-up. My haircut is a bit plain, and my styling skills are next to none, so I decide to give myself a French braid just to make my hair a little more interesting. I throw on jeans, a shirt, and a chunky sweater.

Sierra's bedroom door is open, and I can see that no one is in there. I hear her snoring, though, and it's coming from Eric's room. Passing by Tony's room, I hear him on the phone.

Breakfast is laid out in the kitchen like a buffet. Lifting up the covers to the chafing dishes, I find eggs benedict, bacon, toast, some kind of potato hash, and fresh fruit salad. There's also three different pitchers of juice, coffee and tea set out. I could get used to this. Beats my cereal and cold milk.

"Sleep well?"

Putting back a cover, I turn around to find Eric smirking at me.

I nod, grab a plate and turn back toward breakfast.

"Nice jeans," he says, his gaze staying on my ass even after I've turned around to face him.

I'm wearing my best stretch jeans. Got it on sale at Macy's. I didn't buy it to look sexy, though I know the pair fits me well.

To my astonishment, Eric walks over and puts his hand on my butt. "Not bad for white girl ass."

I jump. Part of me doesn't believe he actually did what he did. I don't know what to do. He's the host. Not just my host. But Tony's, too. I'm essentially in his house, about to eat his food, so a part of me feels impolite calling him out. Maybe I'll just let this instance slide.

"Personally, I'm not a fan of ethnic asses anyway," Eric says, following in my steps. "And small tits can be sexy, too."

I flush. I can hear Lila saying, *I know your mother taught you better than that.*

If I were of quicker wit, I might have a comeback like "just like small dicks can be fun," but I'm still stunned. I'm hungry, but I don't want breakfast now if he's going to be around.

I've reached the corner of the counter, a dead end.

Eric draws up in front of me, invading my space. "You seemed to like that pool table. Maybe you and I can play a round tonight?"

"It's a snooker table," I reply, though what I really want to say is "get the hell away from me."

The next thing I know, his hand is between my thighs, grabbing me. I yelp and manage to scurry away.

"That—that's not okay," I manage to stutter, wishing I had the guts to clock him.

He smirks. "I paid for you, so I basically own your pussy."

"I didn't agree—you shouldn't assume—"

"You know that I can have any pussy I want? We Drumm men, when we see something we want, we take it."

I feel sick now and have lost my appetite. Plate still in hand, I rush out of the kitchen and collide into Tony.

He catches me. "Are you okay?"

Still discombobulated by what happened, I avoid his gaze and mutter, "Yeah."

"Did you have breakfast?"

"I'll eat later."

He looks at my plate and takes it from me. "Why not now?"

"I remembered I have to, um, text my roommate."

I hurry past him and scurry upstairs to my bedroom. I sit on the bed and wrap my arms around myself as if I'm cold. I feel gross, violated, and disappointed in myself. I don't like that I came across so helpless and felt so defenseless. Why can't I be the sort of woman who's quick on her feet, why can't I be more assertive, why do I have to be so timid and weak?

I've read articles about women who've accused Eric's father of sexual harassment. I guess the fruit doesn't fall far from the proverbial tree.

"What the matter with you?"

I look up to see Sierra at my doorway. She's wearing one of Eric's shirts.

"Eric molested me," I blurt.

"What?"

"He touched me, then grabbed me."

Sierra stares at me, then rolls her eyes. "Is that all?"

"What do you mean 'is that all?'"

"Get over it."

"You think it's okay that he did that?"

She shrugs her shoulders. "It's not that big a deal. Think of it as a compliment. Afterall, it's not like he assaulted you or hurt you in any way."

I decide it's not worth talking about it to Sierra. It's only making me feel worse.

"Did you think you were going to be treated like some princess?" she asks. "Hello? You agreed to trade money for sex. What were you expecting?"

Maybe she has a point. Maybe I only have myself

to blame.

But I know I don't want to have to put up with it.

Tony appears, a frown on his face.

"I'm gonna change," Sierra says before leaving.

"I changed my mind about going," I tell him. "I should study."

He doesn't look surprised, and his tone is grim when asks, "What happened?"

The look of burning steel in his eyes makes me hesitate. I want to tell him the truth, but that might put Tony in a position of having to choose between me and Eric, and he's supposed to befriend Eric.

"I was...I was just being touchy about something Eric said," I say.

He raises his brows. "Is that all?"

I nod and put up a fake smile to mask the misery I feel inside.

"Then I'd like for you to come. My cousin Benjamin is meeting us there."

I frown at the prospect of spending time in Eric's company, but if Tony wants me to, I don't want to refuse. I'll just have to make sure I'm not alone with Eric.

CHAPTER TWENTY-NINE

We take a helicopter into Northern California. I get a little motion sick, the feeling sitting on top of the ickyness still in me over what happened in the kitchen.

But it's a gorgeous day, yet another blue and cloudless sky in California. I wish Lila could see the view of the Pacific Ocean rolling into the beaches and cliffs, though Lila gets motion sickness worse than me. Though we're not biologically related—maybe it's possible if we trace our roots back far enough—we share traits like motion sickness when flying, slight gluten and dairy sensitivities, and an inability to hold much alcohol. I remember at one dinner, Lila had a glass of wine on an empty stomach and nearly passed out.

I didn't think I would be ecstatic with having to spend more time in Sierra's company, but I'm thankful that she joins our trip. Eric pays me little attention. I see Tony looking in his direction a number of times.

The helicopter heads east, away from the ocean and into a more rural area, eventually landing in an open field. Tony helps me out of the helicopter. I still feel nauseous and hope I don't throw up all over him. I am very happy to put my feet on solid ground.

"This is at least a four hour drive from the Bay Area," Tony notes.

"Yeah, but we're in friendly territory here," Eric replies, "away from all the liberals of San Francisco and Berkeley. There's an initiative to break up the state of California. Folks here are conservative. They don't have anything in common with the tree huggers and hippies south of here."

"You couldn't find a site near the ocean?" Tony asks.

Eric sighs. "The state is protective of the coastline and preserving what they call open space. But once my dad is elected President, we're going to change that. The federal government will trump state law."

Tony raises a brow. "We studied the US government in a number of my courses in college, about a balance built into the country's Constitution between federal power and states' rights."

"Yeah, states' rights are needed when the federal government tries to impose its will."

"Which is acceptable as long as that will matches your own preferences?"

Eric laughs. "Exactly. America is about winners, and winners get to make the rules."

A large black SUV drives up at that point. The front doors open, and out steps a big fellow who looks like he could be an NFL lineman, and the other one must be Tony's cousin because he's even more of a head-turner.

Eric walks up to greet them. "Benjamin Lee, nice to finally meet you."

Benjamin, who stands a few inches taller than Tony, shakes hands. I see a similarity between the cousins in the shape of their mouths and the width of their brow, but Benjamin's features have a different quality about them and his hair, though still black, is a shade lighter.

Tony introduces me. "This is Virginia."

I shake hands with Benjamin. Sierra is clearly an afterthought to Eric, but he introduces her as well. I can tell she's as struck by Benjamin as I am.

Tony nods toward the large Asian man standing next to the SUV. "You still have to drag a babysitter around with you?"

Benjamin smiles. "And where's yours?"

"Gave mine the week off. No one's likely to try anything here in the States."

"You should be careful after what happened in Hanoi."

"At least it's known there can be consequences when attempting anything on me."

Eric intervenes. "So let me tell you why this is going to be the best resort and golf course outside of Florida."

He proceeds to describe his vision for a two hundred room luxury hotel with a spa and several award-winning restaurants, the 18 hole golf course with views of the hills, and a vineyard on site.

Sierra and I hang back while the man talk shop. She's wearing a thin sleeveless dress and strappy sandals and clings tightly to a shawl while she shivers. I've discovered that the state of California has a lot of different climates, and the one here makes me think of the Pacific Northwest.

"What else is around here?" Benjamin asks.

"Not much," Eric admits, "but we don't need anything else. There'll be golf for the men and a luxury spa for the women."

"You expect people will drive three, four hours out of the Bay Area to come here for golf and spas when they can get that much closer to home?" Benjamin asks.

"Yes, because this will have the Drumm brand. And the Drumm brand is synonymous with luxury and exclusivity. The best of the best will want to come here to play."

Benjamin takes off his coat and hands it to Sierra, whose lips are visibly turning blue despite the amount of lip gloss she has on.

"I've got schematics I can show you over lunch," Eric says. "There's a bar and grill in town that's our best bet. Bill, the owner, is a big supporter of my dad's."

The bar and grill reminds me of Hooter's because all the waitresses have low-cut skin-tight shirts.

"I know this isn't a Michelin star restaurant," Eric explains after we're seated in a corner booth, "but I'm not elitist. This is good old American comfort food, and the scenery's not bad either."

He winks at Benjamin and Tony, neither of whom seem to share Eric's mirth. After we've all ordered, Bill comes to our table. He's about fifty years old, with a receding hair line and a slight beer gut showing.

"Drinks on the house," he declares. He claps a hand on Eric's shoulder. "Think your dad will swing through town anytime soon? Man, I love the guy."

"He would campaign in California if there was a chance of winning the state," Eric replies.

Bill sighs. "Yeah, I tell you, it's them liberals in San Francisco and LA. They're not like the rest of the state. You tell your dad that."

"We know."

"What I like about your dad is that he's a regular joe, like me and other working stiffs."

I find his statement interesting because Drumm has been a billionaire for all but the first twenty some years of his life. Before that, he was 'simply' a multi-millionaire.

"He tells it straight, right?" Bill continues. "And he's a man of action. He wouldn't be a rich man if he wasn't."

Eric and Bill talk politics for a while longer. Bill doesn't pay much attention to Tony or Benjamin until Eric mentions that Benjamin and Tony's families have a combined net worth of over twenty billion dollars.

"We're going to develop a resort and golf course in this county," Eric tells Bill.

"You do that. Bring jobs to the area. God knows the liberals haven't done squat for us out here."

"That's what the Drumms are about: bringing jobs and boosting the local economy."

"Well, I tell you what: anytime you fellows want to have lunch here, it's on the house. That's my gesture of appreciation for what you're doing."

I look around the restaurant. The customers appear to be solid working class people. Of all the people here, Eric, Tony and Benjamin are the last people who need a free lunch.

"You've barely eaten anything," Tony says to me later.

"I don't want it ending up all over the helicopter," I admit, poking at my salad.

"Is it just the helicopter or all modes of flying?"

"The helicopter is especially brutal. I can feel the turbulence."

Tony turns to Benjamin. "We need a ride back with you and Bataar."

Benjamin nods.

"Thank you," I say to Tony.

Knowing that my stomach won't be twisted from the inside out, I finish my lunch. Afterward, I decide to use the restroom. So far it's been kind of interesting listening to the men and even amusing to watch the waitresses trying their best to flirt with them. Eric is friendly, but I'm secretly satisfied that Tony doesn't seem interested at all in the women.

Even though Benjamin Lee is intimidating in his own way, I'm feeling relaxed and have been working on distancing myself from what happened in the kitchen with Eric. What he did was wrong, but I don't want my day to be ruined because of him. That's giving him more power than he deserves. On the helicopter ride up, I was glad that it was hard to have a conversation, allowing me to be in my world for a while to work through all my thoughts and feelings. The arrival of Benjamin was a nice diversion. It's hard to tell how close the Lee cousins are to each other. They didn't greet each other with the openness that Lila or Mo would have greeted one of their relatives, but it could be a cultural thing.

And if Tony and I are getting a ride with Benjamin, I get a reprieve from Eric. I just have to decide if I can stand the rest of the week in his company. Is the money worth it? Is Tony?

CHAPTER THIRTY

It's worth it, I decide.

But then I step out of the ladies' room and walk right into Eric.

"I bet you feel really lucky," he says.

The hall leading to the restrooms is narrow, and I get the sinking feeling that if I try to walk around him, he's going to grope me again.

I don't say anything, hoping he'll get tired of talking to me.

"You see all those waitresses throwing themselves at us?" Eric goes on. "But you and Sierra are the lucky ladies that are going home with us. You notice how jealous the waitresses were of you two?"

One of the waitresses had rudely taken my salad plate before I was done. The others mostly ignored me and Sierra.

Since I think Eric's question is rhetorical, I remain silent. Eric takes a step toward me, and I think about ducking into the ladies' room again, but his arm shoots out, blocking my path and caging me against the wall.

"So how about a game of pool—excuse me, snookers—tonight?" he breathes on me. "I can snooker you real good."

I'm floored. Did he not pick up on the vibes I was sending in the kitchen? Or does he not care? Is he so full of himself that he can't imagine a woman not wanting to be with him?

His other hand grabs my ass. I push his hand away. He puts it back. I swat it away.

"Stop it," I tell him.

He leans in even closer to me. "Playing hard to get, babe?"

I can smell the beer on his breath. He presses his body into mine.

Just then a waitress enters the hallway en route to the ladies' room.

"Oh, is there anything else I can get you, Mr. Drumm?" she asks, batting long fake lashes at him.

Eric grins in response, and I take that moment to scurry away. Once out of the hallway, I gulp in air as if I had been suffocating. I was mostly angry at myself over what happened in the kitchen. Now I'm mostly angry at Eric.

As I sit down at the table, I am aware of Tony's gaze keenly on me. I feel like a deer being watched by a wolf. I'm glad for the buzz of my cellphone, indicating a text has come in. It's from James regarding our planned study session. I don't know what to reply. I had considered texting him to say that I wasn't going to be available this weekend, but now I'm not so sure.

I avoid looking at Eric when he returns. I can't stay at his place, I decide. He makes my skin crawl, he makes me feel ashamed of myself. And I don't want to have to put up with him.

But twenty thousand dollars...

I've already lost three days of work. All that I've done would be for nothing.

Well, not quite nothing. If money wasn't even on the table and I had the option to give up my virginity to someone like Tony, I'd probably go for it anyway.

Still, why did Eric have to screw things up for me? Why did he have to ruin it all? He gives billionaires a bad rap. Or maybe they're all like him. Maybe having a shitload of money makes you feel grossly entitled, like you own the world and the people in it.

I'm glad when it's time to go.

"You don't look well," Tony says to me as we walk to the SUV.

The man named Bataar gets in the driver's seat. Tony holds the back door open for me.

"The salad's not sitting well," I lie. "Probably should have had them hold the blue cheese."

I stare out the window as Bataar pulls out of the parking lot and heads toward Highway 5. As if he knows we're basically just escorts, Benjamin has barely said anything to me or Sierra. Which suits me because I don't feel that talkative.

"What do you think?" Tony asks. "Is it worth

investing in?"

We've been driving for a while in relative silence because Benjamin was on his cellphone. He speaks in Chinese, and I'm struck by the long vowel sounds of the language.

But Benjamin has been off the phone, and when he doesn't answer right away, I look over at Tony to find him staring at me. Surely he wasn't directing the question at me?

"Drumm wants ten million for the golf course alone," Tony says.

I look over at Benjamin, awaiting his response.

"He's asking you, Virginia," Benjamin says.

I start. What?

"Should I invest in Drumm's luxury resort and golf course?" Tony rephrases.

"I don't know anything about business," I reply. Why the hell is he asking me?

"Regardless, tell me your impression."

I realize both cousins are listening to me. I take a moment to think so that I don't come off sounding like a complete idiot.

"I don't know much about the resort business," I qualify again, "and even less about golf courses. But given that there are a lot of options for golfing—in prettier places along the coast—I wonder that people will travel here for that. Unless it's a spectacular one-of-a-kind golf course. I don't know what goes into making one golf course more attractive than another."

"What else?"

"As for the resort component, Eric said the spa would be for the women. As with the golf, there are a lot of options to choose from down near the Bay Area. In other words, there's a lot of competition. Unless the plan is to draw from the population around here."

"Not enough rich people here. The entire county is smaller than a lot of suburbs. Any other considerations?"

"Well, what is your goal? If it's to be buddies with the Drumm family, then that's a consideration."

"I know your father wants those defense contracts," Benjamin says to Tony, "but they'll never let a Chinese company get their hands on anything substantive. Just look at the limitation in the telecomm industry. And the senior Drumm is no fan of China."

"Father knows it's a long shot," Tony replies, "but it doesn't hurt to cultivate a relationship with the Drumms."

I inadvertently clear my throat, making Tony look my way.

"You don't think so?" he inquires.

"No. I didn't say anything. I don't know."

"Let's return to your analysis of the development opportunity. Putting aside the potential political benefits, do you think I should do business with

Drumm?"

Hell, no.

"I can't really say," I deflect.

"Why not?"

"I don't know enough about how he is in business. I've heard things about the family business, how they don't pay their contractors sometimes and that they contract with companies that use undocumented workers. But maybe it's not true. Or maybe it doesn't matter in business?"

"Drumm projects are never on schedule," Benjamin adds, "because they do contract with companies that use unskilled labor, which is cheaper but not as efficient."

"Which is kind of ironic. You'd think a luxury resort would be built by the best workers to be had. Even if the labor drives up costs and you have to charge your customers more, given the type of clientele Drumm wants to target, couldn't they afford the higher rates? Their price elasticity of demand would be less than one—inelastic."

Benjamin glances over his shoulder at us. "You should hire her. If you don't, I might."

Tony stares at me. Hard. "She's mine."

I don't know what to say to that.

"Go on," Tony urges me.

"Well, what do you want in a business partner?" I ask him.

"A proven track record of success. Business

acumen."

"Anything else?"

"Like what?"

"Like honesty. Ethics. Shared values, maybe. I'm assuming you wouldn't want to deal with someone you didn't trust or who was unethical."

Or maybe that doesn't matter if he has connections to the criminal world. Maybe *he's* the one who's unethical and untrustworthy.

"Are you suggesting I shouldn't trust Eric?"

"I don't know him that well," I mumble, looking away.

"What does your intuition tell you?"

"What does yours say?"

"I know what mine is. I want to know what yours is."

I shift in my seat, unsure how to respond. I finally recall, "Mo used to say how you do one thing is how you do everything."

"Which means?"

"It means how you show up in one part of life is a reflection of how you can be in other parts."

"Is there a reason you aren't answering the question directly?"

I blurt, "I think he's an asshole, and I don't think he can be trusted. That's my honest opinion."

I bite my bottom lip, wondering if I was too candid.

Tony looks unfazed. Maybe it's because he's come

to the same conclusion.

Feeling like I need to back up my statement, I add, "The Drumms have been accused of a lot of shady dealings, and though nothing has been proven in court, I've noticed their attorneys never address the questions head on. Instead, they resort to smearing and name-calling their accusers. But I could be misjudging it all. I'm not a business person. Maybe this is normal in the world of business, in which case, I'm glad I'm not in it."

This time Tony looks surprised, I think because of the force with which I spoke. And the heat in my tone is definitely the result of what happened between me and Eric today. He represents all that is wrong with a profession that puts money above people.

"How else is Eric an asshole?" Tony asks.

"You probably deal with assholes all the time in your line of work," I murmur, ready to be off the subject. I don't want to have to relive the reasons I think Eric is a jerk.

"We come across them frequently, and sometimes we don't have the choice of walking away. This can be the case when we have to work with government officials. But I try not to make a practice of working with assholes if I don't have to."

I look out the window at rows of olive trees. I still have to text James back.

"So far I agree with everything she says,"

Benjamin tells Tony. "My first impression of Eric? He's a first order wanker. He's not a complete idiot, but his hubris drops his business IQ significantly. I think the allegations in the news are just the tip of the iceberg."

"But if his father becomes president, those allegations won't amount to anything," Tony replies. "Even if this resort and golf course is a loss, which it probably will be—"

"The water costs alone could sink it. California is a damn desert."

"That hasn't stopped you from investing and developing in the state."

"Our projects aren't golf courses in the middle of the bloody sticks."

"It's a loss we can afford."

"You're inclined to work with Eric then?"

"From what we know of the Drumm family, they are—what is the expression—tit for tat? Scratch a back to get yours scratched."

"You go in on this, they'll be knocking on your door for other investments, like the acquisition of a football team."

"American football is not so bad."

"Basketball is much better."

I perk up at the mention of basketball.

"Don't let your personal biases cloud your financial judgment," Tony cautions his cousin.

"My brother plays basketball," I say.

Benjamin asks about Andre, what position he plays, how long he's been playing. I talk about Andre's potential and the camp his coach wants him to attend. Tony listens attentively.

"His coach thinks he has a shot at a college basketball scholarship," I explain. "Lower level division two, for sure. But if he goes to this camp, maybe a division one school will take notice."

"You have any footage of him playing?" Benjamin asks.

I take out my cellphone and pull up several video recordings, which I share with Benjamin.

"He's good," Benjamin says after viewing the videos. "Abilities on both ends of the court. He looks disciplined on the floor. You said you're from North Carolina? I'm sure the D-1 schools in the area are familiar with him. You do live in basketball country."

"Andre's good, but he's not head and shoulders above the competition for places like Duke or UNC," I reply, "but maybe if we can get other colleges interested, a school like UNC might take a closer look at him."

We veer into other conversations, and I'm disappointed when we're back in the Bay Area. I liked listening to Tony and Benjamin converse, switching seamlessly between English and Chinese. I wonder what it would be like to learn Chinese.

The car pulls up in front of the house, and I look upon it with foreboding. Sierra and Eric are probably inside already.

"It was nice to meet you, Virginia," Benjamin says after opening the door for me. "Let me know what happens with your brother. I might be able to help out. Tony can you put you in touch with me."

"You starting a sports scholarship program?" Tony asks.

My phone rings, and I pick it up. It's Mrs. Ruiz. But even though Benjamin has walked to the other side of the car, I can still hear him.

"You need a reason to stay out of trouble," Benjamin is saying to Tony.

"So I can be more like you?" Tony returns flippantly.

"The family business won't do it for you. Nor will Carmen."

From the corners of my eyes, I see Benjamin look my way. He finishes his thought. "She might."

CHAPTER THIRTY-ONE

"Virginia? Hello?"

I turn my attention back to my call. I don't know what Tony's response to his cousin is.

"I'm sorry," I say to Mrs. Ruiz. "Could you say that again?"

"Are you feeling better?" she repeats. "We're very short staffed this week."

"I am feeling a little better," I say.

"Then are you coming in tomorrow? I really need you."

I think about my job and how I'm letting Mrs. Ruiz down, the studying I'm supposed to be doing, the fact that I don't want to spend more time under the same roof as Eric.

"Can I...can I call you back in a few hours?" I ask.

"Okay, but don't forget."

She knows I'm a responsible employee. Or at least I was before I decided to do this crazy thing of selling my virginity.

Turning around, I wave at Benjamin as his driver pulls away from the house.

"Your cousin seems really nice," I say to Tony.

His pupils constrict momentarily before relaxing. "He's not bad for family."

I hesitate at the threshold of the front door to Eric's temporary home. I didn't want to tell Tony what happened with Eric for a number of reasons. I haven't sorted things out for my own sake, and it doesn't feel like something you confide in with a guy, let alone one you barely know. A guy might be more empathetic to Eric's position and dismiss my reaction as overblown, like Sierra did.

Part of me wants to run and cry to Lila about it, but I don't want to make her fret about me. So my roommate Talia would probably be the one I would talk to. She'd want to kick Eric's balls, and I'm not sure that I'm up for battle mode. Maybe because part of me feels like I'm partly at fault. I was someone willing to sell my virginity to a stranger, so that must send a signal to Eric that I'm a certain type of girl. And even though I can reason to myself that it shouldn't matter what sort of girl I present myself as, a man doesn't have a right to grope me, I still feel oddly guilty.

My feelings don't make sense to me, I don't know how I'm supposed to feel about all this, and I'm just not ready to talk to anyone about it.

But I have to tell Tony something. I have to tell him why I don't want to stay here. And then come up with what to do instead.

Don't just complain, Pastor Johnson likes to say.

Be part of the solution.

"What's the matter?" Tony asks.

I realize he's opened the door and I haven't stepped through.

"I was thinking about work," I reply. "I just got a call from Mrs. Ruiz."

Tony seems to ponder something when Eric shows up. My spine straightens, and my pulse quickens. I stand closer to Tony.

But Eric doesn't even seem to see me and addresses Tony, "I just found out Stephen Antonis is in town. His family was there on the ground floor of Mykonos and Cofu. He's up for having drinks with us, but we'd have to leave in like twenty minutes."

Tony glances at me.

"We should leave the women here," Eric says. "They'd be an unnecessary distraction."

"Are you okay?" Tony asks me.

"Definitely," I reply, glad that Eric will be gone soon. "Go. I'm going to catch up on studying."

Instead of studying, however, I turn over the day's events in my mind over and over again, replaying what had happened in the kitchen and at the restaurant as if I could change what happened just by thinking about it. I'm upset with myself for letting it get to me. I want to be with Tony, but can I endure a week under Eric's roof? Can I take being in his company for a few minutes, let alone several days? Though I have the feeling he would protect me against Eric, I can't expect to be at Tony's side the whole time. Maybe I can see if Tony is willing to stay in a hotel instead. I feel bad asking him to do that, and maybe he'll decline, in which case I have to decide whether to put up with Eric or forgo my chance of earning twenty thousand dollars. Maybe I just need to stand up to Eric. Just like his dad, he probably gets away with all kinds of crap. Someone has to stand up to him. Maybe I can get a shred of my dignity back that way.

I told Mrs. Ruiz that I would call her back in a few hours. I'll tell her I need another day of rest. I feel bad about that, too. But twenty thousand dollars is worth the misery and the guilt.

Actually, that's kind of a selfish way of thinking about it. Mrs. Ruiz doesn't gain anything out of this. She'll probably have to rely on Rosa or Mrs. Park to work overtime. That may or may not be a good thing for my coworkers.

Sierra wanders into my room again, and I try not to groan audibly. She smacks her chewing gum.

"You have fun hanging out with the Lee men?" she asks.

"It was nice getting to know Benjamin," I reply stiffly.

"I was looking him up on the Internet and guess what I came across."

She holds up her large screen cellphone. It's some blog or news column. I see a photo of Tony, his arm around the waist of a beautiful Asian woman. She has perfectly manicured brows and plump rosy lips. She doesn't wear long fake eyelashes, but she doesn't have to. In the picture, Tony is leaning in toward her as if he's about to kiss her or whisper something in her ear. The caption below the photograph as well as the article are in Chinese.

"So this is Tony's girlfriend?" I inquire with a sinking heart.

Sierra looks at her phone. "Oh, more than that. I dropped the text into Google Translate, and here's what it says."

She pulls up a different window on the browser to show me. Taking the phone, I scan the words about the engagement between billionaire developer Tony Lee and Hong Kong actress Carmen Cheong. I stop and remember what I had overheard Benjamin say.

The family business won't do it for you. Nor will Carmen.

This is the Carmen Benjamin must have been referring to. Tony's fiancé. I read more about his visit to Australia, where Carmen is shooting her latest film. I look at the date of the news article. It's dated five days ago.

"Figures a guy like Tony wouldn't be a bachelor," Sierra comments. "Eric would be in the same boat, too, but he just broke up with his girlfriend and is choosing to live up his new freedom for a while."

Tony's a cheater. He has a fiancé. A gorgeous

movie actress. That shouldn't come as a surprise to me that he would have a woman like that in his life. But then what the hell was he doing with me?

I scan more lines from the article, which quotes Carmen as saying, "I couldn't be more in love."

I can't read anymore and hand Sierra back her phone. I doubt that Carmen knows what Tony is up to. And even if she does, I don't want to be a part of some love triangle.

It's not a *love* triangle if it's just *sex* between me and Tony. Which of course it is.

I swallow painfully. Was I really kidding myself that it might be more than that?

"What's the matter?" Sierra asks.

"He never said anything about being engaged."

"Why would he? He probably has different girls in different parts of the world, one for each country. That's how men are."

"Not all men."

My father wasn't like that. He was loving and loyal. I once heard him say to Lila, "You'll always be woman enough for me."

"But men like Tony and Eric are different. You get to their level of success, it's natural to want as much as you can have of anything, including women. Only men who are poor settle for just having one."

I disagree, but it's not a point I'm going to argue with her. I start to pack up my things.

"What? You're leaving?"

"I got a call from Mrs. Ruiz. They're understaffed."

Sierra snorts. "And what's that to you? You think businesses like The Montclair care about our lives? Why should we care what happens to them? I'm sure they're making plenty of money."

I go into the bathroom to collect my toiletries. I know I'm behaving like a jilted lover. And even though there's a possibility that Carmen is fully aware of Tony's side activities, I doubt she's perfectly okay with it. Back in North Carolina, I had a friend whose boyfriend cheated on her with her best friend. She forgave her boyfriend but not her best friend.

How you do one thing is how you do everything, I had told Tony. I don't know why I was so drawn to him. He has a bit of a sketchy past with this whole triad business. Maybe there was more to what happened in Hanoi than he lets on. And now this. The fiancé. It's not worth it. It's not worth the possibility of having to endure Eric's company for the rest of the week.

But what about the twenty thousand dollars?

It's just money. I shouldn't have done this to begin with. I don't regret losing my virginity, but I should get back to the real world, my world. This hobnobbing with billionaires, being paid to be there sexual servant, is not for me.

Grabbing my phone, I look up a local taxi company and call for a cab.

Sierra shakes her head. "You're such a weirdo."

My next call is to Mrs. Ruiz to let her know that I'll be coming in for work tomorrow.

CHAPTER THIRTY-TWO

The cab ride back into the city is going to cost me more than I can really afford, especially given that I've missed work. I have the driver drop me off at the nearest bus stop in the city so that I can shave eight dollars off the trip. I remember that Dan said he would deposit my cut of the down payment into my bank. I'm not sure how much of it he'll let me keep, but it turns out not to matter. I check my bank balance on my app and see no new deposits.

"You're back early," Talia says when I walk through the door. "Thought you had to work late."

"I told my supervisor I had to study for my midterm," I reply, trying to sound upbeat though I feel like shit.

"I've got to leave for my evening class so I'll catch you later."

I'm glad to have our room to myself. I feel too miserable for company. As I unpack, I come across my textbook. Great. Now I won't be able to study without first thinking about Tony. And everything he did to me.

I wonder what explanation Sierra will provide for

my departure. But it doesn't matter. I'm never going to see Tony or Eric again. And that's a good thing.

I spend the rest of the evening with a pint of ice cream and the television, mindlessly watching Disney's *Beauty and the Beast*. It's amazing how timeless fairy tales are. I bet a little girl who longs for her own fairy tale resides in all women. Maybe that's why I let my judgment get clouded. Not that I had any illusions that Tony was my happily ever after, but maybe I thought he could be a temporary Prince Charming. A wickedly, sexy Prince Charming.

My cell rings. Seeing the phone number, I'm filled with dread.

It's Dan.

"What the fuck?" Dan says as soon I pick up. "Where the fuck did you go? Eric wants his money back."

"He groped me."

Of all the people I thought I was going to tell, I did not expect it to be Dan.

"Oh my god, you're kidding, right? That's why you left? What's wrong with you?"

I realize I should have come up with something that wasn't the truth.

"You were going to make thousands of dollars," Dan continues. "You don't need that money anymore or something?"

"I changed my mind about things."

"Jesus Christ. You're fucked up. Even if you gave

up your virginity, don't expect to be paid a cent 'cause you didn't hold up your end of the deal. And now I've got to deal with a dissatisfied client. And not just any client. The son of the guy who could be our next fucking president!"

"I'm sorry."

"You're sorry? You think 'sorry' is going to help?"

I don't have a response. I feel too lousy to consider what I should say.

"Go fuck yourself," Dan grumbles before hanging up.

I put the phone down and almost start to cry. It's never fun to get yelled at, even if it's undeserved. I did screw things up. I'm not sure Dan is someone worth worrying about, but I feel terrible nonetheless.

Again, I want to call Lila, but I'm too embarrassed at the moment. I hug one of the throw pillows and eventually fall asleep on the couch.

I wake up at five in the morning and decide to get ready for work. After work, I'll head over to school and see if I can catch Mr. Parker.

"Virginia, can you come in my office?" Mrs. Ruiz asks just after I clock in.

I skip going to change and enter her office, sitting down across from her desk. I suspect she wants to talk about the days of work that I have missed.

"Virginia, you are aware of our policy about fraternizing with the guests," she starts.

"Of course," I respond.

"And what is that policy?"

"Interactions with guests must be professional at all times."

"Precisely, and you understand this policy? There are no questions about what is considered professional?"

I think about the brief words I have had with Tony at the hotel. Should I not have spoken to him at all? But I didn't initiate the conversations. Or maybe she's thinking of that older businessman who tried to hit on me months ago?

"I don't have any questions," I say.

"I thought you understood as well. You can imagine, then, how surprising it was to find out that you have been...associating with Mr. Lee."

I stare at her dumbfounded. Either she's overreacting to my early encounters with Tony or...

"What do you mean?" I venture nervously.

"One of our employees saw you enter Mr. Lee's vehicle."

"He offered me a ride in his limo to the MUNI station because it was raining. He happened to be there when I slipped in front of the hotel."

"It was not raining in the photo I received, it was not his limo, and it was not near the hotel."

A photo? She had received a photo? I immediately think of Sierra. But then I remember I had also bumped into Tracy.

"Now, normally, this would be grounds for termination."

I look sharply at Mrs. Ruiz, a sick feeling churning in my stomach.

"But given that Mr. Lee is also the owner of the hotel, or his family is, the situation is less straightforward," she continues. "However, if you are a person of character, of integrity, you understand that your actions set a very bad precedent for others and stands in egregious defiance of an important policy. I'm not going to fire you, but I think it is obvious that your continued employment here is to no one's benefit. I hope you know what I consider an appropriate solution."

I draw in a difficult breath. "You want me to quit."

"I do not think you would be happy working here. I had considered you one of our best employees, and it is very disappointing for me that you have chosen to do what you did. If you leave, you are free to pursue your...continued interaction with Mr. Lee."

I almost laugh ruefully, but there's no use explaining to her why I won't be seeing Tony anymore.

"Should I...leave now?" I ask.

"Yes. Your final payroll will be sent to you in the mail."

I can see that she has nothing more to say, so I get up. I walk out of The Montclair, but I don't know where to go because I'm supposed to be at work.

Suddenly, I have free time that I shouldn't have. I wander into a coffee shop to drown my sorrows in a cold swirl of caffeine, chocolate, whipped cream and caramel drizzle. I open my textbook to study, but my mind can't seem to retain anything.

I remember I have yet to text James to confirm a time and place to get together to study. I take care of that and spend the next ten minutes re-reading the same page.

Get it together, Virginia Mayhew Porter. So the last few days ended up in the crapper. It doesn't mean you should bomb your econ test.

I try to focus on studying but give up after fifteen minutes. I take out *Fifty Shades Darker*. But even escapist fiction holds no appeal. Maybe a chocolate chip cookie would work better.

The cookie helps a little. I think the only way I can purge this out of my system is to talk to Lila. I know she'll be there for me. I just have to swallow my shame.

I pack up my books and decide that maybe a walk will help clear my mind. I step outside the coffee shop and stop in my tracks.

It's Tony.

CHAPTER THIRTY-THREE

"Enter the car," he says, opening the passenger door of his Porsche.

I stare at him. How in the world did he find me?

His countenance darkens. "Now."

Feeling it's best to obey, I get in without a word. He starts driving.

"I'm not going back to Eric's place," I say.

"That's not where we are going."

"Then..."

But he doesn't seem like he wants to talk, so I don't finish my question. I guess as long as we're not headed to Eric's, I can stop worrying.

Only he pulls up in front of The Lair.

"Why—what are we doing here?" I ask as the same lady from last time opens my door.

I feel stupid not getting out of the car, so I step out, but I keep my backpack with me in case I need to find my own way to City College.

"Eric's getting his money back," Tony tells me after he hands the woman his keys.

He takes me by the elbow and half drags me inside the building.

I try to dig in my heels. "So what does that have to do—"

He stops and stares at me. "I'm going to give you one last chance to earn the money."

From his expression, I get the feeling he's going to eat my alive.

"Twenty thousand," he specifies, then pulls me inside.

I'm not sure I want this chance. I had reconciled myself to missing out on the money. But I am now out of a job...

"Good morning, Mr. Lee," the same receptionist greets.

On the counter in front of her, on a velvet tray by itself, is the red and black mask I wore the last time I was here.

I don't take up the mask and instead ask as nonchalantly as I can, "Does Carmen know about this?"

He looks at me sharply. "She has no need to know."

"Cell Three is ready as you requested," the woman says cheerfully.

Tony grabs the mask and me, then heads for the stairs.

"I didn't say I agreed to this," I protest.

"You agreed to 'anything and everything.'"

"That was before..."

"Before what?"

"Before I knew about Carmen."

It's early in the day, and the place seems deserted. Tony and I might be the only patrons here.

"What do you care about Carmen?" he asks. "You don't know her."

"I don't have to. I just—I just don't want to be in any form of soap opera."

"And how would that happen? You think Carmen's worried about you?"

I manage to pull my arm from him. "It's—it's...bad juju."

Okay, that wasn't the most sophisticated thing to say, and it's clear that Tony doesn't know what I'm talking about, but I couldn't think of a better response.

I improve in the next statement. "And it speaks to the type of person you are."

He crosses his arms after he gets to the bottom of the stairs. "Which is what?"

I stop on the last step. My gaze is nearly level with his. "A cheater. If Carmen doesn't know what you do, then you're a liar, a deceiver."

"And why should Carmen know?"

His question confuses me, but I reply with the obvious, "Because she's your fiancée. That's reason enough."

My words give him pause. Surely he gets what I'm saying?

He uncrosses his arms and looks almost amused.

"Carmen and I aren't really engaged."

That's an awfully convenient excuse, I think to myself. Aloud, I say, "I saw a news article and a photo. You were about to kiss her—or something."

"That was staged. We secretly broke off our engagement weeks ago, but her grandfather had been thrilled about our engagement. He's on his deathbed, and while he is still alive, we're pretending we're still engaged. The engagement shouldn't have happened in the first."

"I don't believe you."

Tony grabs my jaw and pins me to the wall of the staircase, trapping my backpack uncomfortably against me. "Don't believe me. Believe I'm a cheater and a liar. And those are my nicer qualities. You should run from me, *ma petite*. Run very far."

I might do just that, but I'm still in his clutch. And then his mouth is on mine, smothering me. My senses fill with him, and it's not a bad way to drown.

No! I didn't agree to this yet.

But my body is already warming, already succumbing. And he knows it. Somehow he knows it. He presses his body to mine, and currents shoot up my spine. His mouth plumbs the depths of mine. He's ruined kissing for me. I know I'll be comparing all future kisses to his.

I want so much to pull him to me, to wrap my arms about him and thread my fingers through his hair. But I left him for a reason.

And that reason was?

His engagement.

Oh, right. I'm in trouble.

"I told you, you should have walked away from me," he murmurs atop my lips with anguish. "I was trying to be better. And now...I can't."

His lips still locked to mine, he picks up my legs and grinds himself between my thighs. And I miss this. I miss feeling his ardor thick and hard against me. I kiss him back. My arms encircle his neck, pulling him closer as he dry-humps me.

Holding me by the legs still, he carries me into Cell Three. He kneels on the mattress and sets me down. He cups my face with both hands, and his lips move almost reverentially over mine. I haven't been out of his presence for twenty-four hours, and I'm starved for his touch.

His hands drop to the straps of my backpack, peeling them down my arms. After removing it, he puts it aside on the floor. He wraps a hand about the back of my neck, massaging away the last of my feeble resistance. His mouth takes mine once more, and I wish I had worn something sexier than my flannel shirt, sweater vest and jeans. He looks sexy and dreamy in his button down shirt beneath a beige pullover sweater with the sleeves rolled up. Of course he looks sexiest with nothing at all on...

Deciding I want him in that state, I thrust my hands beneath his sweater and start to unbutton his shirt. That makes him kiss me deeper and harder. Feeling like a horny teenager, I unbuckle his belt and unbutton his pants. My sex throbs. The soreness is practically gone, and I won't be satisfied till I feel him inside me.

He whips off his sweater and sheds his shirt. I happily run my hands over his pecs, brushing over his scar, and then his midsection, down to his crotch. He's wearing boxer briefs. Tight boxer briefs. I rub his erection through the cotton/spandex fabric.

He takes off my sweater vest and pulls open my shirt, sending buttons flying.

"Hey!" I cry.

"Merit your twenty thousand and you can buy yourself a new shirt," he says in between biting my bottom lip.

I had forgotten about the money. "How do I earn it?"

He brushes his knuckles along the curve of my breast above my bra cup. "Make it through...without using your safety word."

Don't do it, Virginia. It's a trap.

"Without my safety word," I echo. "At all? Under any circumstance?"

His gaze hardens with desire. "I told you not to trust me."

He pulls down my bra cup and his mouth latches on to a nipple. It's not fair. He works me up so that I'd do just about anything while exonerating himself because he warned me about him.

God Almighty.

The more he sucks and licks my nipple, the more my better judgment fights a losing battle. I slide my fingers through his thick hair and moan at the pressure on my nipple, at how it seems to send signals to my pussy, causing the wetness to flow.

"Be careful what you choose," he says before pushing my bra over my breasts and switching to my other nipple. He cups my crotch with one hand.

It doesn't even feel like a choice anymore. His rubbing penetrates through my jeans to my clit. He nibbles more aggressively on my nipple. I'm officially a hot mess.

He yanks my shirt off, undoes my jeans, and pulls it along with my underwear down my hips, creating enough room for him to slip a hand beneath my crotch and caress my folds and find my clit.

Yum.

I purr at his fondling. It's so good, I want to come right now. Make me come, Tony.

I stop caressing him because all I can think about is the craving between my legs.

"You want to come, Virginia?"

I practically pant like a dog awaiting its treat. "Yes, Sir."

"Then beg."

"Please make me come. Please, Sir. I would do anything."

"Anything?"

"Anything."

"How about I spank you?"

"Spank me, Sir."

"Flog you?"

"Flog me, Sir."

His fingers have me in a frenzy. I grip his shoulders and remain still as if my life depended on it because the slightest movement might ruin his perfect strokes, his perfect application of pressure, his perfect positioning.

"How about I fuck you?"

"Yes, oh, yes, Sir!"

"Hard?"

"Please fuck me hard."

"How hard?"

"As hard as you possibly can."

"You think your little pussy can take it?

"Yes, Sir. Fuck me till I'm screaming. Then fuck me till I can't scream."

"Mon dieu."

He pushes me onto the mattress, and I fall on my back. He pulls out a condom, tears it open and pushes down his pants and underwear. I think I'm about to get what I asked for. I say a quick prayer for myself.

With the condom on, he pushes my legs, which are locked together by the fact that my jeans and panties are still about my thighs, up and to the side.

My body forms a twisted 'L' position. He points his cock at my entry and pushes in, stretching me, undoing the healing that took place during the reprieve. It's uncomfortable and wonderful at the same time.

I'm grateful that he takes his time and doesn't shove his entire length in all at once. Instead, he withdraws a little, sinks in deeper, withdraws again, and presses in further. Ripples of delight wave through my loins.

"Play with your breasts, your nipples," he commands.

I put my hands on myself and lightly tug at my nipples.

"Pull harder."

I pull my breasts into pointed peaks.

"Nice. Now pinch and twist them."

I follow orders.

"Harder. I want to see tears, *ma petite*."

He demonstrates, making me gasp and cry.

"Your turn."

I try, but self-preservation will only allow me to inflict so much pain on myself. He compensates by slamming his cock into me. I scream loud enough for the entire building to hear.

There's no turning back now. He buries himself to the hilt over and over, pushing my body to its limits, making the safety word so tempting. Only I don't remember what it is! What the fuck is my safety word? I wonder in desperation and panic.

The force of his pounding seems to have no end.

"St-stop!" I squeal.

But that isn't the safety word. He continues with the rough and relentless fucking. He's got his tears now.

"Sir!...Sir!"

He slows, and I gulp in relief.

"That hard enough for you, Virginia?"

I mew. "Yes, Sir."

He pulls out, straightens my legs, and walks over to the dresser, where he finds a vibrator. My body is a single note of hurt, and I'm not sure if the vibrator will do it. He slides it between my thighs and turns it on. My body isn't used to the mechanical vibrations and jerks away, but he presses down on my abdomen, holding me in place as he nestles the vibrator head against my clit. It doesn't take long for pleasure to replace the pain. Soon all that matters is my need to come.

Which I do with another loud scream. I shake against his hand and buck against the vibrator. So beautiful. So awesome. So worth it.

I wait for the chance to sigh with the descent of my climax, but he continues to hold the climax in place.

"Thank you, Sir," I whisper.

My clit starts to protest.

"I came," I tell him louder.

"We can pull another one from you," he replies.

My eyes widen. No way. My clit is too sensitive. This is no longer feeling good.

"Just push through it."

"No, please! Tony! Sir!"

I clench my jaw and shut my eyes. How in the world am I supposed to...?!

But he's right. There is another plateau. The discomfort from the oversensitivity hasn't disappeared, but there's a second wave of pleasure that drowns it out, and it's even more potent than the first. Back arching off the mattress, limbs trembling, I am nothing but spasms. Thrilling, decadent spasms.

The vibrator retreats form my madly pulsing pussy.

He turns it off. "Next time we'll wring three from you."

CHAPTER THIRTY-FOUR

As I lay on the mattress, feeling the blood pulsing and bubbling through every vein in my body, I murmur, "I don't remember my safety word."

I suspect that I'm going to need it.

"Tar Heel," Tony provides as he pulls off my shoes and strips off my jeans and underwear.

Right. How could I have forgotten?

Flipping me over, he unclasps my bra and kisses his way from my shoulder, down my back, to my butt. He caresses and massages the same path with his hands. I release a satisfied breath and close my eyes to soak in his touch. He knows just when to be gentle, when to be firm, and when to be rough. I don't know what he has in store for me next—I know better than to believe he's done already—but for the moment, I am relaxed.

He sheds his shoes and the rest of his clothes. He reaches for a black bag on the mattress, and I assume he's putting the vibrator away in it, but a shot of adrenalin disrupts my hitherto content state when he pulls the bag over my head. I immediately sit up, my hands grasping at the hood, but he pulls on the strings of the bag, drawing it tighter about me.

"Relax," he murmurs in my ear. "You have your safety word if you need it."

I still and try to calm my racing heart. I'm not sure what I thought was going to happen, but I can't see anything through the hood, and for a second I did think he might try to suffocate me. But now that I take a step back from complete panic mode, I realize I can breathe just fine. In fact, I can sense that the fabric about the mouth is not as thick as it is about the eyes.

He's sitting behind me and pulls me to him. I lean back against his chest and try to settle the rest of my nerves. His hands knead my breasts, then caress my midsection. He reaches one hand between my thighs, stroking languidly, tenderly.

"It wouldn't have mattered if I was engaged or not," he says in a low voice, almost to himself. "I had no chance against you."

I'm not sure what he's talking about, so I remain silent. Plus, I don't want to use up too much of the air inside the hood, which is growing too warm for comfort.

"I wanted you too much," Tony continues. "From the moment I saw you."

Really? I knew I was drawn to him but had no idea he felt that way about me at the beginning.

"*Bon sang.* I don't know why."

Me either.

I think about how young I was when I knew I wanted to be with Lila. How could I have possibly known at that age? It was just an instinct.

I was right about Lila, but could I be mistaken about Tony? Is it just my lust talking?

He squeezes a breast and rolls my clit around, making me groan. I had noticed that he hadn't come yet. I can feel his hardness against my backside. The soreness has returned, but my body doesn't care. It wants to come again. It wants to be there for him.

"Do you remember if you preferred the stinging or the thudding sensation?" he asks.

I quietly groan but answer, "I think I liked the thudding."

"Then we'll start with that."

"What?!" Are we doing both?

"A little punishment is in order."

"Why?"

"Because you left without permission, without even telling me where or why you were going. And because you just came, twice, without asking permission to come."

Crap.

He pulls me up to my feet and gently walks me over to a different part of the room. I try to remember what the room contains. Am I next to the cross? The cage?

I hear what sounds like a padlock. My pulse

quickens. Tony bends me over until my neck comes to rest against wood. He sets my wrists on either side of my head. I know which apparatus he has chosen now. It's the pillory. I hear him closing the top of the wood frame over my neck and wrists. I hear the click of the padlock.

I hear him walk toward the armoire and dresser, then silence. He's probably contemplating which of the implements to use. I hear a drawer opening. The suspense is killing me. I want to be able to see, to anticipate what I should brace myself for.

He returns to stand behind me. I'm not sure what implements he's chosen. He caresses my rump, then plays with my clit. When he withdraws, my body is desperate for his touch, whether it's pleasurable or painful. Anything is better than the vacancy.

I hear a whack and realize he's struck his hand with the paddle. I can handle this. I survived his last spanking.

"You've been a bad girl, Miss Virginia."

I swallow with difficulty. "Yes, Sir. I'm sorry, Sir."

"You deserve to be punished."

"Yes, Sir," I acknowledge, happy when he caresses my ass again. I just hope he gives me some warning before he spanks me.

"What is the lesson you need to learn?"

"To ask permission before I come."

With his thumb, he moves my clit from side to side. "And?"

"And not run away."

He doesn't give me a warning, and the paddle sends my shoulders crashing into the stocks. Shit! That was hard!

"How bad are these transgressions?"

"Very bad... Sir"

The second blow makes me gasp so hard the hood is drawn into my mouth. I spit it back out. The air inside has grown even warmer and more humid.

He caresses my burning ass.

"How badly should naughty girls be punished?"

"Very badly, Sir."

"Correct answer," he says before landing another forceful whack.

My legs start to quiver, and tears sting my eyes. I wish I knew how many of these blows he plans. I can maybe last seven or eight more of these. After that, I'll seriously have to consider using my safety word.

"Do you think I should go easy on you because you're new?"

I readjust my number after the fourth blow. There's no way I can take seven or eight more of these. My ass will break apart before then.

"Well, Virginia?"

I whimper, "No, Sir."

I cry and shake against the pillory with his next strike. It's like he's trying to hit a fucking home run on my ass. Maybe I should've responded that I preferred the stinging sensation.

"You should thank me for the punishment I'm giving you."

"Thank – thank you. Sir."

I feel something smooth against my folds. Whatever it is, he rubs it back and forth along my slit, coating it with my juices. It's not the vibrator. It feels smaller. It is smaller. He presses it inside me until my pussy swallows it whole.

I jump when the vibrations start. It was novel enough experiencing the vibrations on my clit, but now they're inside of me. No matter how my body twitches or jerks, it can't escape the vibrations. I start to pant. My legs want to buckle. And then the vibrations stop.

"Hold still," he instructs.

Whack!

The force of it sends me onto my toes and slams me again into the pillory. My lower back feels tired from being in this position. I make a note to myself to do more core exercises.

"Do you like your punishment?"

"Yes, Sir."

"Would you like more?"

It's a trick question. I groan, "Yes, Sir."

The paddle bites into my ass, pushing tears out both eyes. I consider the safety word, but the vibrations are back, making me reconsider. If I use my safety word, there's a chance I won't get to come. And I want to come. I suffered enough. I deserve to come. I want to show him I can do this. I want to meet or exceed his expectations. And the money would be nice, too, if he's sincere about me earning it, but that reward is a secondary consideration in the moment.

He lets the vibrations go for several minutes, letting them build my arousal toward my climax. Yes! This is going to be so worth it.

He spanks me with the paddle while the vibrations are going. Yes, yes!

But then the vibrations stop.

"May I come, Sir?" I remember.

"Not yet. We haven't gotten to the stinging sensations."

I hear him set aside the paddle. A whip cracks the air. I clench my hands and brace my body. To my surprise, it doesn't sting as much as I'd feared. Back and forth, it smacks one buttock, then the other. In the same manner, the whip travels down my thighs, slapping one side, then the other.

But that was just the warm-up.

There's a break in action, an ominous pause before the whip slices across my bruised and battered bottom. I shriek. He whips me again. God Almighty!

The vibrations return, making the next several falls of the whip more bearable. But I wonder how much more I can take?

The whipping stops. A minute later, I feel his legs

behind mine. His cock is at my opening. Before I can remind him about the vibrator thing inside of me, he pushes into me.

O. M. G.

I'm beside myself with both the vibrations and his cock filling my pussy. He thrusts gently, but it's enough to send me into another galaxy. I can't *not* come.

"Pl-Unh! Pl-Sir—"

What falls from my lips is a garble of pleas and grunts as he thrusts harder, shoving me into the pillory. It rattles continuously as he pumps into me, smacking his pelvis into my rump, renewing every ache and every sting. I begin to rethink the possibility of suffocating in the hood. It's so damn hot and humid, and the air becomes thinner with every gasp and groan.

But what matters most is the pressure cooker inside of me. I think he must have a hand on the pillory because he finds more leverage with which to slam himself into me. His other arm holds me up, preventing me from crumbling. I've got to come, but I can't get the words out.

"Not yet," he warns.

I actually choose to focus on the pain, of him ramming into the pillory, of how much my ass smarts, of how much I hate the hood.

"Come, Virginia."

His words are heaven-sent as I shatter into a

thousand pieces. Euphoria sings through every pore, every vein. It's more than I can take. I've devolved into a bundle of nerves, and I don't know that I can be put back together.

God Almighty.

CHAPTER THIRTY-FIVE

"How did you know where to find me?" I ask as I curl into Tony on the mattress.

Somehow my body is intact, in one piece. I'm sore between the legs, and I won't want to sit down for a while, but I feel surprisingly invigorated.

"Your BW2T app," he replies, his arm wrapped warmly about me.

"But how—did you use the app to spy on me?" I try to imagine how that is possible.

"You had your location services enabled in that app, and hacking into BW2T wasn't that hard."

"You hacked into BW2T?"

"Not me personally, but the tech firm we invest in employs hackers to test their security."

"It's kind of creepy that you would hack into my phone."

I make a mental note to either disable location services in that app or delete it altogether.

"How else was I supposed to find you? I went to The Montclair looking for you, but Mrs. Ruiz told me you had quit. Why did you quit?"

I hesitate before answering, "It seemed awkward

to work there given—you know. And I violated hotel policy."

"*I* violated the policy. You didn't initiate anything."

"I don't think that matters."

Tony lets out a long breath. "Do you want your job? I can get it back for you."

"I'm sure you could, but I can find another."

"You won't need a paycheck for the time being. I'll have the full twenty thousand wired to you. It should show in your account tomorrow."

So his offer was for real? He's not lying like Dan did?

"I'm sorry," I say.

"Why the fuck are you sorry?"

"If I had finished the week, you wouldn't have had to pay. Eric would have."

"I don't want that *connard* to have anything to do with you."

"I don't either," I murmur with lowered lashes.

Tony cups my jaw and turns my gaze toward him. "Why did you not just tell me?"

"Tell you what?"

"What happened with you and him."

Wait, is he assuming Eric and I...? Did Eric lie and maybe say I came onto him?

"Nothing was going on between me and Eric," I insist, disgusted with the idea that I would want to come within ten feet of Eric if I had the choice.

"I know it was not *that*. But you thought I could not sense something was wrong?"

"I didn't want to mess up your business goals with him. And I didn't want to talk about it."

Tony puts his hand to his head and looks up at the ceiling. "Well, *ma petite*, you did 'mess up' the plans."

I frown and bite my lower lip. "I did?"

"I can't work with the *salaud* after what he did."

"How do you know what he did?"

"I confronted him when I returned to find you gone."

"Maybe he's different in business. And his dad could become the next president of the United States."

"*Baise-le*. Fuck Eric. Fuck his dad. You think a man could lack integrity in one area of his life but be honest and good in another? You told me how you do one thing is how you do everything."

"But..." I furrow my brow. "...does it really matter to you?"

"It shouldn't," he replies with surprising emphasis. He shakes his head. "I feared I would ruin you, but you're the one who's ruined me."

"I didn't mean to! Is there anything I can do—I'm not going to bring charges or anything against Eric. I don't think anything would come of it if I tried. You could still do the deal with him."

"He's lucky that all I did was tell him to go fuck

himself. Nobody touches what is *mine*."

"Oh. So that's it. It's not that what Eric did was wrong. It's that he did something to *you*."

Tony stares at me with that familiar intensity of his. "Yes."

I stare back at him. It's like he's daring me to be angry, which I should be if I truly believed my own words.

"You want me to believe the worst in you," I realize, sitting up so that I can see him more fully.

"I'm no good for someone like you."

I think for moment. "You could have just let me believe you were engaged to Carmen."

"Is that why you left?"

"Is that what Sierra told you?"

"She said she didn't know why you left except that you mentioned you had to study."

"I didn't want to be 'the other woman.' I mean, what kind of person would I be if I knowingly had an affair with another woman's man?"

"But that's what happened, no? You don't believe that I broke off the engagement. And maybe you're right: maybe I didn't. Maybe I lied. I lied so I could fuck you one last time."

I shake my head. For some reason, I feel more confident in my intuition. "You're not as bad as you think you are or want to be. I couldn't like you as much as I do if you were."

A corner of his mouth curls. "You like me, do

you?"

I flush. "Isn't that obvious?"

"*Je suis baisée*," he murmurs.

"What does that mean?"

"My father and brother are going to be—what is the best word—pissed?"

I don't think he's really answered my question. I'm convinced his words in French were more about me than his family, but I let it go. "I won't be upset if you changed your mind about working with Eric."

His face darkens. "It's done, Virginia. If I see him again, it's to break his nose."

I look away. "I'm sorry—"

He sits up in a quick, fluid motion. Clearly his core muscles are in much better shape than mine. He cups the back of my head and draws me to him till our foreheads touch.

"If you say 'sorry' one more time, your punishment is going to hurt so badly—"

I suck in my breath and blurt, "Sorry—"

With a groan, he crushes his mouth to mine. The world spins, as it always does when he kisses me. I know, even without the twenty thousand dollar enticement, that I would choose to be with him. I may not be the brightest or the most sophisticated woman, but I trust my instincts when it comes to Tony. There's still a lot for me to learn about him, but for now, I am his to ruin.

BONUS

Thank you for your purchase of this book! Sign up to receive a bonus scene by clicking the link below:

https://windcolorpress.activehosted.com/f/105

OTHER WORKS BY EM BROWN

<u>His For A Week Series</u>
Bought
Ravaged
Tormented
Devastated
Ruined

<u>Erotic Contemporary Short Stories</u>
Damien
And Damien Makes Four

<u>Cavern of Pleasure Series</u>
Mastering the Marchioness
Conquering the Countess
Binding the Baroness
Lord Barclay's Seduction

<u>Red Chrysanthemum Stories</u>
Master vs. Mistress
Master vs. Mistress: The Challenge Continues
Seducing the Master
Taking the Temptress
Master vs. Temptress: The Final Submission
A Wedding Night Submission
Punishing Miss Primrose, Parts I – XX
The Submission of Lady Pennington

Chateau Debauchery Series
Submitting to the Rake
Submitting to Lord Rockwell
Submitting to His Lordship
Submitting to the Baron Serial
Submitting to the Marquess
Submitting for Christmas
Submitting for Christmas: The Epilogue

Other Stories
Claiming a Pirate
A Wicked Sea
A More Wicked Sea
Force My Hand

AUDIOBOOKS
https://books.erotichistoricals.com/hot-audiobooks-copy

Excerpt

His For A Week
BOUGHT

CHAPTER SIX

Ben didn't bother changing out of his dark colored suit and indigo dress shirt. His morning meetings had run longer than anticipated, and he didn't want to arrive much later than Jason would. He needed to be there to make sure his cousin didn't do anything stupid with Jake and Derek.

Ben's jet landed at Weaverville Airport, where his rental was waiting for him. After putting his bags in the Jeep rental, he drove himself to the cabin. With its rugged landscape of heavy forestry and the Klamath Mountains, the area was beautiful. Unlike most years, the terrain was verdant with flora as a result of the heavier-than-usual rain in the spring months. Ben had put down the top of the Jeep to bask in the early summer sun, glad to be in dry and temperate Northern California instead of muggy and hot Beijing, where his parents lived.

At the cabin, a stocky man named Vince opened the door. At 6'2", Ben stood taller than most of his friends, save for the ones playing in the CBA, but Vince was easily a head taller than Ben. He didn't know why, but the first thought Ben had on meeting Vince was whether or not he could take the guy out. He was confident he could. Men with Vince's build tended to be slower and less agile.

Jake appeared in the foyer. "Benji, glad you could make it."

The hairs on Ben's neck curled. Had Jake just called him *Benji*?

"Only my mom and sisters ever call me Benji."

"Oh, hey, no problem, brah."

"Where's Jason?"

"He and Derek are coming up together, and their driver got lost. You like bourbon? I was about to open up a bottle of Kentucky straight. It's uncut and unfiltered."

Vince offered to take Ben's bags up to his room, the last one on the left upstairs, so Ben followed Jake into the great room with floor-to-ceiling windows that looked out onto the lake. Jake walked over to the bar, but Ben stopped at the threshold.

At the left end of the room before the fireplace knelt two women. One was a blond in a tight pink faux leather dress. The other was completely naked. Both of them looked disheveled.

"What the fuck?" Ben let drop.

"I see you found my acquisitions," Jake drawled as he opened the bottle of whiskey.

Ben met the eyes of the blond. She glanced down as if not wanting to be caught looking. The other woman stared at him with what seemed like defiance and suspicion. His gaze did a quick sweep of her figure, and his groin tightened of its own accord. She had nice B-cup breasts with dark chocolate areolas, a smooth stomach that led to swollen hips and a cute patch of curls between shapely thighs.

Her left cheek appeared a little discolored and swollen. Her hair was partially and unevenly straightened, and her mascara had spread below her eyes as if she had slept without taking her makeup off.

Jake handed him a glass of bourbon. "You missed out, man. There were prime pickings last night."

Ben glanced at the women again. For women who wanted this shit, they didn't look too happy at the moment.

"Do you have the portfolios I requested?" Ben asked Jake.

"Yeah, but you really want to talk business right now? You just got here."

"Now's as good a time as any. Better. We don't have to bore Jason and Derek."

"Fine, fine."

Jake went to sit at a table before the window. He gestured to the manila folders. "They're all right here. You'll want this guy, though. Jamaal Dixon. He's playing in the EuroLeague right now."

Ben set his bourbon down on the table and leafed through the portfolios. When transacting business, he preferred not to drink. It was hard enough keeping his mind on business with two women, one of them naked, kneeling just yards from where he sat.

"They just going to kneel there the whole time?" he asked, trying to keep his gaze off the naked one—especially her tits and pelvis.

"That's what slaves do," Jake replied as he poured himself more bourbon. "Whatever I tell them to do."

"Why is one of them naked?"

"Oh, that was her preference."

From the corner of his eye, he saw the young woman stiffen.

"What about the one from UCLA?" Ben asked. "Coach saw him at an exhibition game and likes the way he plays."

"You'll have to pay good money for Tyrell Jenkins. He could have been a second-round draft pick if he didn't have that sprain late last year."

They talked about the merits of the different players and the salary each was likely to command. The discussion went slowly because Jake had had three shots and wasn't too focused on business.

"Give Tyrell a call," Ben said.

"I don't know that he'd consider going off to live in China."

"Have you asked him?"

"No."

"Then feel him out."

"Okay, I'll feel him out."

Ben waited.

Jake stared back. "What? Now?"

"Now."

Jake's whole body seemed to curl. "Fine. Since you sound like you're in a hurry, Benji."

Ben gave him a hard look. "Only people with pussies call me Benji. You got a pussy, Jake?"

"Chill. I just forgot."

After Jake pulled out his cellphone and wandered back to the bar to add ice to his glass, Ben sauntered over to the women. The blond looked really young. Like she was barely legal.

"How long have you been kneeling here?" he inquired.

The blond didn't answer and continued to stare at the rug that probably didn't provide much cushioning from the shiny hardwood floor. The other woman glanced over to Jake before answering, "Three hours."

Three hours. Jake was a bigger asshole than he'd thought. Ben played around with heavy BDSM, but he had never made a woman kneel for three hours straight.

"You got a name?"

Again, the blond remained silent.

"Apparently, we're Slut #1 and Slut #2," replied the naked one.

She said it as if it was his fault she had a name she obviously didn't like. She didn't like him, either. Ben sensed that right away. A porcupine was less prickly than her.

"Tyrell didn't pick up, but I left him a message," Jake said as he walked over with his shot glass refilled. "No use talking to my slaves. They're not supposed to talk without my say so."

Ben raised his brows. "And they signed up for this?"

Jake rolled his eyes. "They're getting compensated a shitload of money for their time. Plus, they get to live out their *Fifty Shades of Grey* fantasies."

"How much do they get?"

"I don't know exactly. I paid just over a hundred thousand for blondie and the black girl."

The blond's stomach growled.

"Are you hungry?" Ben asked.

Jake grabbed his crotch. "I fed her this morning."

The prospect of food made the blond look up.

"If they've been kneeling here for three hours, they're probably hungry. Don't you feed your slaves?"

"Sure. I just—it wasn't lunchtime yet."

Ben looked at his watch. "It's past noon. Get them something to eat."

Jake stared at him in disbelief. Ben could tell he wasn't making any friends ordering Jake about, but he wasn't interested in being the guy's *brah*.

"You *are* the host," Ben added.

With a discontented snort, Jake walked over to the expansive Tuscan-inspired kitchen, opened up the well-stocked refrigerator and pulled out a brand-new jar of pickles. Walking back, he set the jar on the coffee table near the women.

Ben crossed his arms. "Open it."

"They're not incompetent." Jake nodded to the blond. "Help yourself to some pickles, slut."

The blond reached for the jar and tried to twist the cap off. Jake had already stalked off to the bar, so Ben took the jar from the blond and twisted the cap off for her. She reached in eagerly for a pickle.

"Just Slut #1," Jake called from the bar. "I'm not happy with the other one."

Ben looked at the second woman, expecting her to hang her head in disappointment. Her stomach had rumbled, too. Instead, she seemed to expect Jake's response. Her jaw tightened and her eyes flashed.

"How come?" Ben inquired.

"She wouldn't eat her breakfast." Jake smiled as if listening to some silent inside joke.

Ben looked at her cheek again. Though her skin was darker than what Ben was used to assessing, the discoloration in her cheek was definitely the beginning of a bruise. "So you hit her?"

"I didn't hit her. What do you mean?"

"Her cheek." *Dipshit.*

"What about her cheek?"

"It looks swollen."

Jake shrugged his shoulders. "I didn't notice anything. I'm gonna go see if Vince went to pick up some lunch."

After Jake had left and while the blond was finishing off her third pickle, Ben turned to the older woman. She looked to be in her mid-twenties. She also looked intelligent. He had noticed her studying him, sizing him up. He sensed she was a little on edge but didn't want to show it. Only when his gaze dropped to her naked body—he couldn't help but look at those inviting curves—did she show any discomfort. When his gaze went back to her eyes, he read their message loud and clear.

Fuck you, they said.

"Just got a text from Derek that they're almost here," Jake announced upon returning.

"How much for her?" Ben asked. The words were out of his mouth before he could think on them.

"What's that?"

"How much? I want to buy her."

Available in print at Amazon, Barnes & Noble, and Kobo

Printed in Great Britain
by Amazon